CAPTAIN SATAN:
PAROLE FOR THE DEAD

CAPTAIN SATAN ™
KING OF DETECTIVES

PAROLE FOR
THE DEAD

By William O'Sullivan

ALTUS PRESS • 2019

PUBLISHING HISTORY

"Parole for the Dead" originally appeared in the April 1938 (Vol. 1, No. 4) issue of
Captain Satan magazine. Copyright © 1938 by Popular Publications, Inc. Copyright
renewed © 1965 and assigned to Steeger Properties, LLC. All Rights Reserved.

CHAPTER 1
ONLY THE RICH DIE

THE RAYS of the afternoon sun crimsoned the great studio window and threw a checkerboard pattern over the luxurious penthouse living room. In a large easy-chair, a dark, sleek-haired, impeccably dressed man stirred and shaded his gray eyes with a gesture of irritation.

"Damn it," he said in a low voice, "I've been sitting here— doing nothing—for three hours."

From beyond the rare Chinese screen at the far end of the room came a discreet, almost inaudible answer:

"Three months, Mr. Adair!"

Cary Adair turned his head sharply, the sun etching his clean-cut features clearly, emphasizing the strong chin, the chiseled nose, the slanting forehead of the man. "What's that? What did you say, Jeremy?"

"I said—" The voice behind the screen materialized, became a spare, somberly-clad individual whose serene face was contradicted by his wide humorous mouth. Aquiline nose, high, intelligent forehead, long jaw, unfathomable eyes; all these were in strange contrast to that wide, mobile mouth.

But most remarkable of all were the long, thin, sensitive hands that the man raised in a motion of explanation when he answered Cary Adair's question.

"I said, Mr. Adair—it's been three months, not three hours."

Cary Adair grunted and came out of his chair with surprising agility for a seemingly indolent man; a man who was the very model of the rich, bored, man-about-town… a man who had 'Gentleman' and 'Clubman' draped in every line of his faultlessly cut dark suit; whose gleaming shoes reflected disuse and idleness; whose strong, well-kept hands bespoke a body without a soul… a sword without an edge.

He strode across to the window and stared down at the

The tommy-gun
spoke its piece.

sparkling panorama of New York Bay, far below. "Make me a highball, Jeremy. Light."

Below him also, but hidden from view by the wide terrace that circled the penthouse apartment, were the teeming streets of New York's financial district. It was a whim that had led Adair to build his home atop one of New York's business skyscrapers… and the fact that he'd had to buy the building to do it hadn't deterred him.

His manservant, who filled the offices of valet, chauffeur and butler with rare competence, was coming toward him with a tall, amber-colored glass on a silver tray, when the tinkle of a musical gong struck gently through the silence.

"The private house 'phone, sir," Jeremy murmured as he presented the drink.

Adair nodded absently as he raised the glass to his lips. "I'm not in, Jeremy."

"Yes, sir. I mean—no, sir." Jeremy set the empty tray on a priceless table and glided noiselessly across the rich Turkish rug. He lifted one of the two telephones in the room. "Mr. Adair's residence," he said in a flat, mechanical voice. Then, a moment later:

"Indeed, Mr. Adair *is* in! Won't you come right up, sir?"

Adair turned from the window with irritation hardening his eyes to an opaque gray. "What the devil, Jeremy? I told you—"

"Mr. Desher, sir," Jeremy explained briefly.

"Oh!"

Jo Desher, Chief Agent of the Federal Bureau of Investigation, was sole possessor of the 'open sesame' that swung the portals of Adair's home inward, at any time. Well, *almost* any time....

Adair drained his drink. His face was perceptibly lightened when he passed the empty glass to Jeremy. The eyes of these two men, master and servant, met in a long look of query and speculation.

Jeremy stood for five seconds after a second gong sounded through the still room... a deeper, more vibrant *bong* than that

4

first one. Then a lazy smile broke across Adair's good looking features.

"Don't keep Mr. Desher waiting, Jeremy," Adair murmured.

The tall, morose butler fought back the ripple of mirth and excitement that played across his mouth. He went to the door with a swiftness that was surprising.

Adair stood with his back to the window, his hands thrust into the pockets of his jacket. He could hear Jeremy's "How are you, sir?" and Desher's rumbled "Okay! Okay, Jeremy! How are you? Busy as ever with your do-nothing boss?"

And the servant's murmured answer, "Not *quite* as busy as—er—at some other times. Your hat and coat, sir? Thank you."

And the next moment the portieres of the room were thrown aside as by a stormy wind when the dynamic chief of the F.B.I. swept through them.

"Hi, Cary!"

"How are you, Jo? Good to see you again!"

Desher—squat, powerful, dark, round of head and with a gleaming, honest light in his brown eyes—stuck out a pudgy hand to grip and shake that of the rangy, debonair, graceful Cary Adair.

IT WAS a strange friendship that existed between these two, but a friendship that was sincere, nevertheless. Meeting casually some nine years previous, Desher had formed the habit of dropping in on Adair from time to time to discuss some particularly puzzling case on which he was working. Desher flattered himself that he brought the breath of adventure and excitement into the life of his apparently indolent friend.

Silent for the most part during Desher's problems, an occasional question on Adair's part would serve to clarify some point for the investigator, bring to his eyes a gleam of grudging admiration that one so idle could be so incisive, could think so clearly.

Adair waved to a chair with a lazy gesture. "Park the frame, Jo. Sit and have a bit of a drink with me." He nodded in Jeremy's direction without looking away. "In the big city for long?"

Desher seemed uncertain. "Yes and no. I dunno. All depends." He sought a chair, his eyes taking in the rich furnishings of the place with combined envy and derision. "Pretty soft for you, Cary—all this." His hands made rising spirals at the magnificence of the surroundings, "All this, and not a drop of work or effort to show for it."

Adair smiled lazily, but he didn't answer until Jeremy had served the drinks. He sipped slowly, then: "We can't all be swashbuckling adventurers, Jo. It takes all kinds to make a world, you know—the rich and the poor, the idlers and the workers, the criminals and the sleuths. By the bye, Jo—how's the detecting business doing?"

A frown crossed the serious face of the F.B.I. chief. He guzzled at his drink eagerly, then set the half-empty glass on the table at his side. "That's what I'm up to see you about, Cary. Something's doing."

Adair's eyebrows went up. He averted his eyes as if to hide

the excitement that had sprung alive in them. "I don't think you came all this distance from Washington to see *me*."

"Not altogether," Desher admitted. "Got to see my local agents about a—death." He paused, his eyes curious. "It's funny how talking to you often clears up my mind on cases, Cary. Like—er—Well, we might as well be frank about it. Like that job that faced us three months ago."

Adair nodded. "Yes. I remember your telling me about it the last time you were here. But, Jo?" His voice was gently joshing. "Didn't you tell me that your mythical 'Captain Satan' cleared that up for you? And left you with the credit and the glory and a raise?"

Desher grunted. "Yeah. But look here, Cary—don't go calling that human devil, Satan, a 'myth.' It's true not many people know of him, fewer yet have seen him. The underworld knows of him as a freebooter, a pirate who preys on their 'big shots' and wrecks them after he gets their swag. The Law knows him as a freebooter who beats the Law itself to the punch."

"Hm," Adair mused. "But—he's not a criminal, Jo?"

Desher shook his head emphatically. "A one-man police force who makes monkeys of us and takes his pay from the crooks he smashes. But still it isn't good. He brings the police and the federal men into contempt. And he isn't legally empowered to do the things he does!"

Desher reached for his drink. The table at his side was empty. He blinked, looked to his left, stared down at the floor on either side of his chair. "What the—?"

Adair leaned forward solicitously.

"Something wrong, Jo?"

"My drink! I didn't finish it, did I?"

Jeremy coughed discreetly. "Isn't this your glass, sir?"

Desher turned, looked to where Jeremy was pointing. On a small table directly next to him stood the half-filled goblet. "Where did that come from?"

"Scotland, sir," Jeremy murmured. "The best imported whisky, sir."

"No, no. I don't mean the whisky, I mean the glass!"

"Tiffany's, sir. They have admirable crystalware, sir."

"Skip it, skip it," Desher growled. "Damned if that was there a moment ago." He drained the drink and passed the glass back to Jeremy. "Funny, every time I come here, I seem to lose my memory!" His eyes drifted back to Adair. "Where was I? What were we talking about?"

"About your mythical Captain Satan," Adair reminded him. His eyes flashed a look of half amusement, half reproof, at Jeremy. "That will be all for now," he told his servant.

"Oh, yes." Desher sat forward in his chair, all interest again. "I tell you, Cary—Satan *isn't* mythical. He's real flesh-and-blood. He's not a newspaper character, I grant you. We can't afford to let word of his activities become widespread. And the average man on the street would hardly believe the story even if he were to hear it."

Adair interrupted. "Well, Jo—you should know about him. You say yourself he has saved your life more than once. And certainly he seems to have been more of a help than a hindrance to you. What's your complaint?"

"Damn it," Desher exploded, "what do you expect us to do? Sit by and twiddle our thumbs while Satan does our work and laughs at us?"

Adair shrugged. "Find the man, if he annoys you so. Find him and put him out of mischief. You must suspect that you know him, at times. It isn't possible that you've seen him face-to-face and *still* don't know who he is."

"The few times I've seen him at close contact, he's been masked," Desher excused himself. "Or at night, in a poor light. He was unrecognizable anyway." He stopped, his face breaking into a delighted smile.

"You'd be surprised if I told you the man I suspected him to be—on one occasion!"

Adair shook his head slowly. "Who? One of your own men?"

Desher's eyes roved over the elegant living room again and he chuckled audibly. "No, not one of my own men, Cary."

"Who, then?"

Desher waved his hand negligently, the smile still on his face. But it vanished slowly with his next words. "Never mind that part of it, Cary. It was too ridiculous. Let me tell you instead what I'm here about, this time."

Adair spoke without raising his voice. "Two more drinks, Jeremy." He smiled apologetically to Desher. "I'm a better listener with a glass in my hand, Jo. Care for a cigar with it?"

Desher nodded as Jeremy slid into the room with two more glasses. He felt in his pocket for a cigar, frowned suddenly. "Now, where the devil—?"

"Your cigars, sir?" Jeremy murmured as he set the drinks down. "You put them in your hat when you came in, sir."

"What? Why, that's nonsense. *I* put cigars into my hat? Do you think I'm crazy?"

"I can't discuss that, sir, in my position," Jeremy murmured as he vanished through the portieres into the foyer. He was back in a moment with Desher's fedora, proffering it to the man.

There, resting on and strongly contrasted with the blazing orange lining of the hat, were an even half-dozen of wicked-looking black cigars.

Adair stared down into his drink when Desher's mouth fell open in astonishment and his eyes bulged. The F.B.I. man rescued his cigars and jammed them back into his pocket, keeping one out.

He bit the head off it savagely and jumped when Jeremy flashed a flaming match for his light.

"This place is haunted," Desher growled, as he puffed the smoke alive.

WHEN HE had the thing going and had exhaled several clouds of gray blue smoke, Desher crossed his stumpy legs and settled deeper into his chair.

"It's nothing we can put our fingers on, Cary," he began. "Just a routine check-up. But a strange thing has been happening to some noted criminals, of late. Especially Federal criminals—men who have been convicted by Federal prosecutors for crimes against the government. Kidnapers, counterfeiters, smugglers, and the like."

10

Adair nodded and sipped at his drink. But he didn't interrupt. Desher continued:

"Well, some of those men have been dying in jail. Under peculiar circumstances."

Adair frowned and sat forward. "Let me get this, Jo. You are investigating the fact that some of the country's most notorious criminals are dying? But—?"

"I know," Desher cut in. "What do we care? Well, for one thing, we keep a pretty close eye on our big prisoners. For another—if it's possible that these men are being wiped out, in jail, by someone who fears that they might squeal, for instance, or that they still have a grip on their particular portion of the underworld—we want to know that, too."

"The circumstances?" Adair asked tersely.

"The notorious Sam Klami," Desher recited. "Killed in an explosion—practically unrecognizable. He was working at a machine in the jail shoe shop. In some way, the machine he was operating exploded."

Adair nodded. "Klami had plenty of money, I understand. Who next?"

"Joe Mikkle, the counterfeiter. And there *was* a boy who had the rock salted away. Worth a million, at least! Mikkle was literally cut to ribbons—his face, anyway—in a prisoners' riot." Desher paused.

"Then, Siggy Murrah; 'King of Smugglers,' as they called him. He was working as a trusty in a prison hospital and in some way had his face horribly burned by ether. He died almost instantly."

11

Adair sat forward, his eyes narrow and gleaming. "How was identification made, Jo—*if their faces were all badly damaged?*"

Desher puffed his waning cigar for a moment then waved a deprecating hand. "Forget that, Cary," he said flatly. "They were the right men. We checked them through the best possible of checks. Fingerprints being impossible, or other identification missing, we checked them through their teeth. Their dental work tallied exactly with our records."

Adair sat back, the light dying from his eyes. He thought for a long moment. "I read that Denver Phil Gilkane—the dope ring leader—was just plain 'sprung'? That right?"

Desher nodded. "Yep. Out of Atlanta Penitentiary. No death there. Why do you ask?"

"Just wondered."

The two sat in silence for a long time. Desher was the first to break it. "Siggy Murrah died two days ago." He grinned mirthlessly. "Burton Murnell can't be shedding any tears over that."

Adair's eyes asked an unspoken question as he reached for a cigarette. He lighted it and sat back again.

"Burton Murnell is the greatest prosecutor of our time," Desher recited a fact that they both knew. "When Murrah went to jail, he swore he would get out and kill Murnell. Screamed it in court—told it to the reporters when he went through the gates—yelled it down the cell blocks every night. Of course, the Federal 'pen' at Lewisburg, Pennsylvania, isn't like some kid's bank that you can crack with a hammer. Still, it's liable to get a man nervous—that 'I'll get sprung and kill you' talk. So Murnell can't be weeping any!"

Adair nodded and rested his head against the back of his chair, his eyes going shut. After a few minutes Desher sat forward and stared keenly. "Hey! You asleep?"

Adair opened his eyes and smiled slowly. "No. Not sleep. Just—thinking… trying to hitch this thing up with—" He paused and sat straight, reaching for his drink. After he had drained it, he said:

"Jo, there's something of a pattern in this thing. Do you get it?"

Desher shook his head, his eyes puzzled. "Pattern? You mean, a similarity? Sure, I see it—they're all prisoners; and they're men who were ring leaders. I told you that. Maybe—just *maybe*, mind!—their old outfits, or competitors, are trying to put them away; shut them up and get them out of the way for good."

Adair shook his head. "I don't mean that, Jo." He smiled suddenly, a gleam of amusement in his eyes. "Maybe Satan's doing it," he whispered in mock earnestness. "Captain Satan!"

"Cut the kidding," Desher growled. "What is this pattern you're talking about?"

Adair sobered. "Just this," he said slowly and distinctly. "Each and every one of those men you mentioned—including the one who escaped, Denver Phil Gilkane—each and every one of them had something else in common, Jo. They were all rich—still rich, despite the fact they were in jail. Don't you see, Jo?

"Only the rich criminals have died!"

13

CHAPTER 2
THE DEAD CARRY GUNS

T HE RAYS of the fading sun cast eerie shadows across the room. Adair's hushed voice, with its almost whispered conclusion, brought Desher sitting on the edge of his chair. It was a weird tableau, a ghostly effect, that held them in a breathless silence for several minutes. Something sinister seemed to have come into the room, to have cast its spell over these two men.

Then Desher stirred, mopping at his brow. "I see what you mean," he said a bit unsteadily. "But still, I don't see what significance it has."

"You don't?" Cary Adair seemed puzzled for a moment, then snapped his fingers suddenly. "I knew I would think of that other thing in a moment! Ever hear of an outfit called 'The Jungle Escape Company'?"

"The Jungle Escape Company?" Desher echoed. "No. What about it? What is it?"

"It was," Adair recounted slowly, "a daring, almost unbelievably nervy group of men who formed themselves into a corporation for one and only one purpose—the liberation of prisoners from the Devil's Island penal colony!"

Desher blinked. "What? You mean—?"

"I mean this band joined together for the express purpose of springing prisoners from Devil's Island, that almost escape-proof French jail in the most hellish and inaccessible part of the tropics. Their operation was simple enough. They would select rich convicts, go to their families or gangs—and for a stipulated price guarantee to set free the prisoner."

"Can't be done," Desher snorted. "Why, it's a crazy idea!"

"Crazy or not, they *did* it! All the criminal's people had to do was lay the dough on the line. The Jungle Escape Company did the rest. No fuss or feathers. If they failed to deliver, the money was turned back."

Desher stared his incredulity. Adair read the look and smiled. "I don't ask you to take my word for it, Jo. Look up the records. Ask one of your friends at the French Embassy. Maybe that'll convince you."

Desher shrugged and sat back. "Maybe you're right, Cary. But I can't see that it has any bearing on this thing I'm working on. We have had only one clean case of escape. And a guard was guilty of that."

"A guard usually is guilty," Adair admitted. "Laxity, or downright bribery. But it's just possible, too, that someone very clever and very thorough could be working to release *our* big-shot crooks. And that *would* be serious. Look at the slap in the face to law and order, to justice! Look at the effrontery, the boldness, that it would invite in other criminals—if such a thing were going on?"

Desher shook his head and laughed slightly. "No, Cary. It doesn't hold water. A good story—yes. But, hell, in this case, our prison systems are too well built, too well calculated to prevent escapes! And then you have the fact that our dead men *are* dead men. How are you going to explain that?"

"I'm not," Adair shrugged, "As I said, it just struck a familiar chord. Both in jungle escape epics and in your story of sudden death in the prisons, the criminals involved were rich—tremendously rich."

Desher looked around and Adair raised his voice slightly. "Two more drinks, Jeremy." He smiled at his F.B.I. friend. "If I'm any reader of signs, Jo, you're ready to leave, but you'll have a nightcap before you go."

"Right," Desher grinned agreement. "I'm in accord with you there."

The talk shifted to small chat on current events, and when they fell silent over their drinks and night crept into the room, Adair summoned Jeremy to turn on a few lights.

"And you might turn on the radio," he added.

"Yes, sir."

A few minutes later the strains of music from a popular orchestra were adding the final touches of ease to the atmosphere that had been so strained only a short time before.

It was when Desher was rising to take his leave that the music snapped off with a startling finality, midway through a tune. An announcer was on the air, breathless. A voice said:

Special news flash! Burton Murnell, famed prosecutor, was murdered in his office a short time ago. Thus the great district attorney follows in death Siggy Murrah, so-called King of Smugglers, whom Murnell sent to jail and who, in turn, vowed death for the brilliant Federal lawyer.

This special newscast comes to you through the courtesy of—

Desher choked off an oath. Adair was at the radio and snapped it into silence.

"Murrah's gang!" Desher snapped in a hard voice. "I've got to get to the Federal Building right away!"

"I'll go to the street with you," Adair volunteered soberly.

AS THEY went down the private elevator that led to the street level from Adair's penthouse, Desher shook his head and smiled, his mind off the sudden development that called him to duty.

"What in the devil brings you to live in an office building?" he asked.

"Oh, are we going into that again?" Adair sighed. "It's the best view of the Bay in the entire city; it's quieter at night than any other section of town you can think of; the streets deserted, the sounds of traffic stilled—and it's the most central point in the city. In five minutes, I can be headed for Long Island or for New Jersey." He paused and grinned. "Besides I'm right above the banks, and it's easier to get to them and get my daily exercise… cutting coupons!"

Desher grunted. "You're telling me! Pretty soft life, I'll say!"

They were at the street level, and Desher led the way. Adair

17

nodded in answer to the respectful salute of a uniformed attendant in the great office bidding. Through the milling crowds, they made their way to the street and to Desher's parked car. The F.B.I. man stood a moment before he climbed in.

"Well, Cary, I won't be seeing you for a few days, at any rate. But as soon as this thing is cleared up. I'll—"

Something hissed past the two men, between their heads… a something that *clacked* noisily against the window of the automobile and fell with a clatter to the pavement. They looked.

"A knife!" Desher gasped. He stared around him quickly, but there was only the hurrying crowd. "Who do you suppose—?"

Adair had backed up to the car, his eyes keened to right and left. In the doorway of the building, coming out toward them, was Jeremy, the manservant. His master looked over at him as he ranged up.

"Well?"

"Just a hunch, sir," the man said in a low voice. "Something impelled me to follow."

The eyes of the two clung for a grim moment, then Adair motioned with his head to the sharp-bladed stiletto that was still at their feet. Jeremy frowned, then leaned down to pick it up.

"Leave that!" Desher snapped. "We haven't a chance in a million of finding who threw that. Not here, we haven't. But there may be fingerprints." He had a handkerchief out, picked it up by the blade end gingerly and wrapped the handle carefully in the folds of the linen. He put it in his pocket.

"Well, Cary? That was a close one, wasn't it?"

Adair yawned, his eyes veiled. "Too close, Jo," he murmured. "I'm headed for a fishing trip, and I wouldn't have had it interrupted for the world."

Desher grunted as he got into the automobile. "Here I have a big case on my hands, and you—*you're* going fishing!"

In another moment he had shot away from the curb with a wry smile.

Back in his apartment, Adair dropped into a chair and thought for some time. He looked up to find a cigarette—and gasped.

On the table in front of him, handle wrapped in a handkerchief, was the razor-bladed knife that had so narrowly missed him and Desher only a short time before.

"Jeremy!"

At the stern voice, the servant came from behind the screen. "I thought it was an unusual knife, sir," he said apologetically. "That peculiar bone handle, sir. You saw it? Real ivory, if I'm not mistaken."

"Well?"

Jeremy shuffled, shifted from one foot to the other. "I—er—thought Mr. Desher would be too busy with his present investigations to give it much thought at the moment, sir. Possibly you might wish to—er—give the matter a bit of thought yourself. Besides—" He paused.

"*Well?*"

"I heard you say we were going fishing, sir. That knife—it might prove useful in—ah—cleaning fish."

Adair's face broke into a quick, broad smile. But he sobered suddenly and sat in contemplation for five minutes. At last he moved.

"Before we begin our… trip, Jeremy," he said, "there are a few things I want done! I'll make a list of them, turn it over to you."

"Yes, sir."

"Get packed, Jeremy. Plenty of money, as usual. We may be gone for a long time. Arrange for our—er—guides. The usual instructions. Lay out my clothes, notify the superintendent, and so on."

"Right, sir."

The servant left. Adair fell into somber speculation, pacing the floor at intervals, at others throwing himself into a chair and puffing at a cigarette nervously.

But when Jeremy came into the room some time later, Adair was composed, his face set, his eyes filmed, opaqued, hardened. He called for pen and paper, scribbled some hurried notes. Later he passed an envelope to Jeremy to be sealed and disposed of.

In another hour, the Venetian blinds of the place were down, and dust covers were over the furniture. In the impenetrable black of the room two men moved with the light-footed swiftness and silence of cats. A ray of light showed momentarily when the door to the private elevator opened quickly, then shut.

Blackness and silence tenanted the penthouse apartment of Cary Adair.…

IN THE center of a group of milling federal operatives in the office of the late Federal Attorney for the Southern District of New York, Jo Desher looked at a cryptic note that he held in his hand… looked at it for the twentieth time. It was in a brutal hand and read:

I told you I'd get you. You thought you were too smart for me; but this proves it… you weren't!

The flourishing signature at the bottom of the note said: *"Siggy Murrah."*

For the twentieth time, Jo Desher stared at the note. And for the twentieth time he explained to his assistant, Carter Colley, "Murrah wrote this a long time ago, Carter. His gang got Murnell, planted the note."

"But the date?"

"To-day's date, sure. But that's easy. The note probably wasn't dated when it was written. They dated it to make it look good. And that ratty gang of Murrah's handled the assignment perfectly."

Colley didn't seem impressed. "The experts say it was written in the last five hours… and Murrah's been dead two days. They also say it's Murrah's writing. How do you answer that one?"

"Damn it, Carter—" Desher checked his wrath when another operative came forward, passed a blank envelope.

"This was delivered a moment ago, sir. Message was, 'It's important.'"

Desher growled his thanks and tore the flap with nervous fingers. He plucked the single sheet of paper from inside it, his eyes going back to Carter Colley. "You see, Carter, there are a lot of ways—"

He paused, his eyes on Colley. But his assistant was staring with rapidly widening eyes at that sheet of paper which his chief held in his hands. Desher looked, too. Looked and gasped.

There, scrawled crudely in ink, was the device of the Satanic figure that they had come to know and to fear… a Satanic figure with pitchfork raised in an attacking position. The emblem with which Satan, *Captain Satan*, announced his entry into the field!

"Captain Satan's back," Desher said in a dead, choked voice.

CHAPTER 3
RENDEZVOUS WITH DEATH

A LONG, sleekly black limousine slid to a stop near an East River pier. Two occupants stepped down from the rear of the car and melted into the shadows of some deserted warehouses.

The car slipped noiselessly down the street and then swung into an alley. In another moment, the driver was out and walking rapidly back, the car safely concealed. The other two stepped out to meet him and the trio made their way swiftly across the deserted street and into the darkness of one of the piers.

A weird, high cry, as of a sea gull, came clear to them. They halted. The tallest one of the three men answered it in kind. After a pause, this latter man called softly, "S-M."

A chuckle came from the dark beyond them. "Hi-ya, Slim! Who are your friends?"

The husky, powerfully built man who had driven the black car answered: "K-O." But before the challenger could greet him, a third voice cut in—hard, cold, and with a touch of savageness in it.

"Captain Satan!"

The guard's voice recoiled. "Oh! Cap'n. I didn't know. You don't usually come with any of the crew. I mean—"

Satan had recognized the man's voice without the necessity of his having had to give his 'emergency' letters… the first and the last letters of the aliases under which Satan's men were known to one another. "Chop it short, Soapy," he snapped. "We have important business here tonight, and not a minute to lose."

"Right, Cap'n." A light played on the trio apologetically as the guard, Soapy, followed his routine… brought into prominence the masked faces and the figures of the three who stood there.

Kayo, the driver, a slight, wing-like mask over his broad-set eyes, grinned cheerfully, flattening more than ever the broken nose that was spread across his apparently Greek face.

Slim, Satan's chief lieutenant, stood tall, almost gaunt, his face immobile and his eyes unfathomable behind his mask. He finished rolling a cigarette by the light of the lamp, his long, lean fingers making the necessary movements at rapid and sure speed.

Captain Satan stared back into the light unblinkingly, his firm chin jutted out, his hands jammed into the pockets of his lightweight coat. Satan's figure didn't bulk nearly so large as Kayo's, but there was a hint of tremendous strength in the breadth of his shoulders, in the columnlike legs to which the close-fitting black trousers clung tightly. On his head he wore a narrow-brimmed, flat-crowned soft hat that was fitted close—seemed all the closer in that the hair which should have showed under that hat didn't show… had apparently been shaved off.

"Right, Slim and Kayo. Right, Cap'n," Soapy passed them.

The three filed in, that same gull cry preceding them into the dark interior, where it was answered again. And then the whole of the far wall of the dank, foul-smelling place jumped alive with a brilliant light that flashed at Satan's hip… a light that speared a group of six men who stood there… men who were masked, clad alike in severe black clothing.

And above the group, clearly outlined against the wall, was the Satan-with-spear device that blanched the cheeks of the 'Law' and brought a quake to the knees of criminals the world over.

"Greeting, Satan's Crew," the leader intoned solemnly.

"Greetings, Cap'n," four of the men answered in chorus. But the other two were silent, seemed to shrink together as the light bored on them.

"We have two new brothers with us tonight," Satan continued, the light never wavering from the pair huddled together. "And one old member recently come back from abroad—Pat." The light danced back to the veterans against the wall, picked out a ruddy-faced little man with a carroty mustache; a man whose eyes twinkled merrily back into the rays of light that were bent on him.

"Nice to be seein' you, Cap'n," Pat said with just the touch of a brogue.

Satan's features relaxed in a smile. "Thank you, Pat." Then

the smile turned off as if it were quicksilver. He said, "Slim! These men been coached? They know what to expect?"

"Right, Captain."

"Roll call and then the initiation, Slim."

The gaunt man stepped forward to bring himself into the light. He looked at a piece of paper he held in his hand. "Doc."

"Here." A man of average stature, calm and dignified, stepped forward.

Slim scrutinized him closely. "Okay, Doc. Gentleman Dan?"

Captain Satan

25

"Here, Slim."

A smile etched the corners of Slim's mouth as he scrutinized the tall, suave man with the waxed mustache and patent leather hair. "Have any trouble convincing the Missus you were going to a lodge meeting?"

There was a general laugh from the crowd, but Satan stirred restlessly. Slim noticed and speeded up the business at hand. "Big Bill?"

"Here." A masked man whose bulbous, shiny nose looked like an ad for a saloon, stepped forward. Slim's eyes twinkled.

"Not drunk, are you, Bill?"

"Same answer as ever, Slim. Two drinks would throw me. I hate the stuff."

Slim nodded and turned to Satan. "Soapy's on the door, Kayo with us. All present, Captain."

Satan motioned the others to line up. "We've two members to be initiated tonight, men," he said solemnly. "We'll get it over speedily as possible." His voice was mild but full of meaning when he added, "We have most important business to be disposed of, and the sooner we tackle it, the sooner we're through and home again. *And the sooner the crooks are smashed!*"

There was a stirring among the men as he spoke, a stirring as of a storm wind plucking at the branches of sturdy trees. At a sign from Satan, the two masked men, who were standing slightly apart, moved forward.

SATAN STARED at them intently for a few moments, then slowly circled the men, his keen eyes ranging over their frames. He seemed to be cataloging them in his mind, etching every

26

detail of their stature and posture in his brain. At length he stepped back.

"What is your purpose here, strangers?" he asked, intoning the ritual of the crew.

"To become blood brothers," they answered in unison, but with a tremble in their voices.

"Why?"

"To join with the others of Satan's Crew in fighting Satan's appointed enemies; to obey orders implicitly; to maintain the secrecy of our order and to refrain from attempting to discover the identity of other members; and to defend to the death ourselves, our brothers and our identities."

Satan nodded and added drily, "And to share in the profits when we smash the crooks. Names, Slim?"

Satan's lieutenant stepped forward. "This one" pointing to a fat, jolly-faced man who was beaming at Satan now, "This one I called The Dutchman. The other—" the smaller man shifted nervously and tried to keep his hands still—"is Solly. The Dutchman has been a soldier, a sailor, a brewmaster's assistant, an insurance salesman, and a dental laboratory worker. College graduate, but too lazy to do anything about it."

Satan stilled the laughter with a raised hand. "The Dutchman is going to prove useful. How about our friend Solly?"

"Tried to be an engineer; ended up as a machinist, welder, lighting equipment trouble-shooter, radio worker."

Satan nodded. "Right, Slim. Now—you new men, Solly and The Dutchman—Slim explained to you the purpose of our work. You know the financial arrangement… one-third of the profits and all the expenses are mine. You men share and share alike on the balance. I—"

Solly interrupted, "It's only right, ain't it? You put up the capital and the brains, you *should* get a big cut, huh?"

"*Silence!*" Satan thundered at the ripple of laughter that spread through the crew. "You, Solly—when I want your approval, I'll ask for it. Hold your tongue until I'm through speaking."

Solly shrugged apologetically and spread his hands. "All right, Captain."

"Cap'n," Satan barked. "Slim is the only one who calls me 'Captain.'"

"Right, Cap'n."

"That's better. Now, you know your emergency call letters?" Both men nodded and murmured their letters—the first and last of their respective names. Satan shook his head.

"Won't do. Solly and Soapy have the same letters. Change Solly's name to Sol, make his call letters *ess-ell*. Make The Dutchman's *tee-dee;* then there won't be any confusion with Gentleman Dan's."

"Right, Captain."

"You, Doc—check these men from head to toe. Weight, height, color of eyes, scars—if any."

"Done already, Cap'n. I even took their blood types. That's a sure check against anyone trying to impersonate them."

"Good idea. Now, Slim—the fingerprints. In blood, as before."

Slim stepped forward quickly, seized Sol's right hand and jabbed a needle into his forefinger. Sol gasped slightly, but was easy to print when the rest of the jabs were made. Each finger was imprinted firmly on a paper that already contained Sol's pedigree. Once, a man had tried to masquerade as one of Satan's crew. He hadn't lived to regret it; hadn't, as a matter of fact, lived any more at all. Doc followed behind Slim, dabbing the fingers with antiseptic.

Slim got The Dutchman's print rapidly.

Satan addressed them again. "None of you men are known to the others," he said tersely. "But *all* of you are known to both Slim and myself. You understand that when we are working on a job, you are to be available for a call by night or day. Don't leave your 'phones for even a minute. Or, if you must leave, you will contact Slim and let him know where you can be reached. Understood?"

"Right, Cap'n," the new members said.

"You were fingerprinted in blood for a good reason," Satan said soberly. "You must shed blood—your own, if necessary—to stay in this group; so you must shed it to join us." His next words were cold: "And I don't need to tell you the fate that befalls traitors, do I?"

The silence was answer enough. Satan turned to Slim. "Check out the equipment to the men—guns, ammunition; money for expenses. And hurry. *We're riding tonight!*"

There was a grim silence, until Slim dealt Sol his equipment. The new member of the crew stared his unbelief at the packet of bills that was thrust into his hands.

"What's this? The pay-off already, huh?"

Satan stared at the little man with the big nose and the

stooped shoulders, then joined in the general laughter. "Watch Sol's expense sheets, Slim," he said when he was turning away.

At the exit of the barren place, he halted, spoke low but crisply.

"We're going to—er—our destination in two cars," he said. "Kayo will drive one, Slim the other. In each car you will find shovels, picks and ropes. We will remove these from the cars when we get to… where we're going. Keep your guns where you can get at them quickly."

There was a hush of excitement over the crew as Satan paused.

"We're going to a cemetery party, men—and I don't want it to be *our* cemetery party! Unless I'm the most mistaken man in the city tonight, this job we're on now is one that's loaded from stem to stern with danger."

CHAPTER 4
CORPSE CARAVAN

FIVE SHADOWY figures wove slowly through the network of headstones and mausoleums in that Long Island cemetery, stooping low to avoid being silhouetted against the far streetlights.

There was a pause while one, tall and agile, inspected at close range a grave marker. He peered, then crept close to the group.

"Getting warm, Captain! It's down this row."

Satan nodded. "Slim! You sure the boys are posted right? One at the gatekeepers' lodge—the other four hidden near the cemetery boundary corners?"

"Right, Captain."

Satan shook his head. "I've got a funny feeling, Slim. Almost a hunch. Let's work fast and get this thing over with."

Slim shivered. "It's giving me the creeps, too, Captain. I'm all for speed myself." He stepped out faster, making his way directly down the row. A little further on he paused again, inspected another marker.

"Here it is, Captain," he whispered tensely. He read from the marker: '*Samuel Klami—Died....*'"

"That's enough," Satan cut him short. "Pitch in, men. And work fast!"

Kayo, The Dutchman and Doc emerged from the gloom and loosed the topsoil with spades. Within two minutes, working as a trained team, they were stacking dirt in twin mounds. Satan hissed a warning when The Dutchman's pick clicked loudly on a stone. After that they discarded the pick and worked only with spades and shovels.

The Dutchman grunted his surprise, a bit later, when his spade struck something solid. "Better work around it," he said briefly, when he had recovered himself. "I seem to be making all the noise—but I struck it that time!"

Ten minutes later, using a pinch bar, they had ropes under the casket and were raising it. Slim fumbled at the outer coffin, once the heavy burden was above ground.

"I can't seem to get a space to pry it open," he muttered, his hands feeling around for a juncture.

Satan threw him a heavy packet. "Really, Slim! I thought you

31

had better judgment than that. Use that drill and open up a pry-hold."

Slim clucked his embarrassment; but he was at work instantly. In five minutes, the pry-bar was snouting into the crack. There was a splintering crack when the wood gave, and the group froze into immobility. Like five statues, they were, as they crouched low and scarcely breathed. Satan was the first to move.

"Crack it," he said grimly. "Two of you get over toward the lodgehouse, in case the watchmen hear anything. If this job is going to be noisy, it's going to be noisy. But it'll be fast, too!"

The Dutchman took the pry-bar from Slim and swung his weight to it. The cracks that followed sounded like explosions to the ears of the tense men. Slim and Kayo eased down toward the entrance gates, their eyes keened into the darkness.

Satan, Doc and The Dutchman made quick work of the remnants of the casket container. Satan whistled his surprise when he saw the cheapness of construction of the box that was within.

"Funny," he murmured, "I always thought big shots in the criminal world made a habit of being buried in the most expensive caskets built! This should be a cinch—and I'm almost sorry that it is."

Doc was tying a handkerchief across his nose. Satan and The Dutchman followed his example. The new member of the crew waited for the sign from his leader, then grimly attacked the inner box. It gave way with a splitting sound.

Satan's lamp sprang alive and focused on what was inside… a still, fully dressed figure in men's evening clothes; but with

Benny the Fog stood rooted in fear and the hooded circle grew smaller.

gloves on the hands, and a cloth drawn tightly about the face and ears and neck.

"Burned," Satan said. "God, Doc—I hate to do this! But we've got to get those teeth. Got to see them and examine the bridgework."

Doc winced; but he nodded, tight-lipped, and drew the cloth from the corpse's head. A moan came from The Dutchman at the disfigured thing that was revealed. But Doc forced his hands to be calm and pried at the teeth that grinned up at him from that lipless face.

The jaws wouldn't move at first, then five teeth, strong on an immovable bridge, fell on the stiff bosom of the evening shirt. Doc was reaching for them, The Dutchman tugging at an arm to bring the "thing" into easier position.

Suddenly the corpse came half erect in the casket—all but the head!

And a voice snarled at them, *What the hell is this?*

The Dutchman pulled away with a sob, jerking wildly at the thing that was in the casket. "It's holding me!" he moaned. "It won't let me—" He stumbled and fell heavily to the ground.

A deafening roar sounded from nearby, and The Dutchman swarmed to his feet. Satan was crouched low, shooting at a nearby headstone. Doc had dropped on all fours and was crawling to flank Satan's target.

"The corpse!" The Dutchman croaked. "The corpse! It spoke… and then tried to hold on to me!"

"Get your gun out!" Satan barked as he aimed and fired again. "Someone crept up on us while we were working!"

"Behind that headstone?" The Dutchman asked weakly. But he made no move to draw. Instead, he watched Doc circle swiftly, saw the gleam of moonlight on gunmetal when Doc aimed, watched with dazed eyes the savage spurts of orange that speared from that gun.

There was a scream of pain… then silence, except for feet

thudding, farther down the cemetery road. Kayo and Slim panted up.

"Step on it, Captain," Slim panted. "The watchmen are coming!"

They started to run; but Kayo paused, stared back. "It's The Dutchman," he growled. "Standing there like he's in a trance!" He ran back, grabbed at the new brother-in-arms, and dragged him along.

At the eastern wall of the cemetery, Soapy joined them, having been on lookout there. "What the hell!" the little man gaped. "What broke?"

There were shouts from behind, the flash of electric lamps searching them out.

"Scramble out," Satan barked. "Get going. I'll cover here and meet you at the cars!"

The crew swarmed over the iron fence, using the ladder which they had left there. When they were safely over, Satan followed and kicked the ladder back into the bushes. He dropped to the ground and sped down the wall and across into a clump of trees where the two fast limousines were hidden.

Gentleman Dan and Pat had already started the motors throbbing under the long, gleaming hoods. Sol came panting up from his post near the watchmen's house. The crew swarmed into the cars, The Dutchman and Sol piling into Satan's, where Kayo took the wheel.

Slim guided the car that carried Gentleman Dan, Pat, Kayo, Soapy and Doc. But Satan leaned out and barked an order at the front car.

"Doc! Get in this car! We're going to split up, in case of a chase, and I want you in here!"

When Doc was transferred, the cavalcade got underway, sliding swiftly and noiselessly through an open field to a far road. Shouting sounded somewhere far in back of them when they came carefully through a fenceless ditch and lurched onto a broad highway.

Slim's car swung right and tooled rapidly into the black night. Kayo twisted the wheel to the left and sped toward New York.

Satan was just sitting back comfortably when Doc struck a match to his cigarette. Sol stared at him, then his eyes swung to the silent, trance-like Dutchman. The little fellow's pupils dilated in the flare of the match. Satan sat up. Light contracts the eyes; fear dilates them.

A piercing scream came from Sol... and another... and another. Satan struck him savagely, knocking him from his seat. Sol snuffled and babbled from where he lay on the floor; but he had stopped screaming.

"The arm," Sol sobbed. "The arm! He has an arm!"

Satan swung as Doc stabbed the ray of his pocket flash at The Dutchman; and both veterans gasped.

The Dutchman, his eyes glassy and straight ahead, clutched in his right hand a naked human arm... an arm that had loosened from the shoulder. Doc leaned forward and grabbed the thing... and laughed aloud.

"Wax!" he said shortly. "It's wax!"

IT WAS a taut group that huddled close in the East River warehouse that was the headquarters of the Satan Crew. It was a weird sight… those eight men crouched close, sitting on the floor, while the leader towered high over them.

Satan's lamp, with the Satanic figure pasted on the lens silhouetted on the wall behind the men, threw a dim light over the crew. Satan was speaking…

"…So here is what we have: Klami's supposed corpse is a wax figure. The Dutchman proved that when, in his terror at that voice which seemed to come from the casket, he tore way and took that arm with him. "Yet"—he showed the removable dental bridgework that Doc had pried from the dummy's mouth—"these are Klami's teeth. Let me hear some ideas."

Slim spoke first. "They're not Klami's teeth. If they are, why isn't Klami with them?"

Satan nodded. "We'll check on that with his dentist, Dr. Leedrum. Doc has already got me that information… Klami's dentist, as well as the dentists of some others I am interested in. But if they're not Klami's, then whose are they?"

Gentleman Dan spoke after a short silence. "Klami has been dead two months. Suppose that Klami isn't dead at all? Suppose that in some way Klami had been sprung, had been loosed from jail, and another body substituted for Klami's? With Klami's teeth!"

Satan smiled. "You're thinking straight, Dan. But then why didn't we find a *body* in that grave instead of a dummy? Why isn't the *body* that was supposed to be Klami's in that coffin?"

Doc said, "That's easy. If any question comes up after the alleged burial of Klami, and the authorities exhume the corpse, they *might* be able to prove that the corpse wasn't Klami at all.

But with a dummy? There's no way that they can prove that it wasn't Klami who was killed."

Satan's eyes glowed through the slits in his mask. "Right! And the answer to that one is… Klami doesn't care what they find, so long they don't find that other corpse. Therefore, Klami—assuming that he is alive, has had a 'break' engineered for him—is somewhere that he knows the authorities won't ever find him. In Europe, South America, anyplace. And the corpse that was supposed to have been Klami has been disposed of… for all time!"

Big Bill had different ideas, though. "Sounds good, Cap'n. But you don't break out of jail like a circus dog going through a paper hoop. Just how was this thing managed? How did they get that—that other Klami into jail and the *real* Klami out of jail?"

"Right," Satan agreed. "And that's what we're going to find out—maybe! I took a long gamble on my theory, men; a long gamble. It started when I heard that Burton Murnell had been killed… *after* Siggy Murrah was supposedly dead. Murrah hasn't been buried yet, so I couldn't check on that. But I could check on some other rich criminal who had died—supposedly died—in a like manner.

"*If* that thing that we found in the coffin to-night had been the real Sam Klami… then I was never wronger in my life. But I wanted a quick answer and I got it. How this thing is being worked, I don't know. If it's what I believe it to be, it's one of the cleverest bits of staging ever perpetrated."

"Suppose it is what you think it is?" Kayo asked. "What are you going to do about it?"

Satan's smile was cold as death. "Take people who plan and execute these breaks are taking terrible chances, Kayo. Terrible chances. There's only one thing that would move a man to take such a chance—a whale of a price! But they can get it. What's a half-million to a millionaire crook—who knows he'll never get out to spend it? Nothing! But it means plenty to the man who can engineer it. And the crook who has a million will gladly give half to get out. He still has five hundred thousand when he's free." Satan paused.

"Multiply that half-million—or whatever the price is—by four, by five, by six! Then you know how much it's worth to the men who are working this thing. It's big game, I tell you! And big game that's a menace to United States' justice. If *one* criminal can be sprung, *all* criminals can be sprung... for a price. That means murder, robbery, rape, arson, kidnaping—every crime on the calendar!—can be committed, and the criminals can be sprung if they have the price. *And be free to do it all over again!*"

He looked at the men about him.

"*Now* do you see what this game—what the *breaking* of this game, means?"

"Suppose you had guessed wrong, Cap'n?" Gentleman Dan smiled.

Satan shrugged. "I'd have felt pretty cheap. I think that even a crook has a right to peace in his grave—if there is any peace for him. But Klami has bothered too many people in his life for me to have any respect for even his body." He gestured with his hands. "And I was sure I would find something. But I'll admit I expected to find a corpse—to have to prove that it wasn't Klami's. I'm glad I didn't."

The crew sat in silent contemplation for some moments, turning over in their minds the immensity of the thing—the daring, the cunning, the ruthlessness of it. And the danger. A mob capable of engineering a thing like this would be rich, powerful, elusive; and, cornered, perhaps the toughest thing that Satan's Crew had yet encountered.

"All right, men. Attention to orders."

SLIM STOOD and came to his chief's side. It was to him that Satan spoke, though for all the others to hear. The group listened attentively, every eye on the leader as he spoke.

"That graveyard was being guarded to-night… watched, anyway, from inside. Why? Klami's mob, or the crowd behind these jail-breaks, is watching to see if they are suspected. I want that cemetery to be covered, to see if a new guard is posted—in case that dummy corpse is buried again. Maybe the watchmen will call the police. But it's more probable that the gang behind this will get to the watchmen, keep the thing quiet! They can represent it as gang revenge; the desecration of a corpse; any-thing. Maybe the fact that it was a dummy in that coffin hasn't been discovered, even yet.

"And I want a man sent to Joe Mikkle's grave—outside Philadelphia, I think it is—to see if there is a secret watch posted there, too."

"Right, Captain."

Pat cut in with, "Cap'n? How do you know that man who opened up on you in the cemetery wasn't a copper, a detective? Or a cemetery guard?"

Satan sighed. "I'm not warring on the police. The man who came up on us fired when he saw that I spotted him nearby. A copper would have covered us. A cemetery guard would have covered us, or sent for the police. That man was a torpedo, a gunman." He smiled grimly. "If I'm wrong, we'll know by the morning papers! But it's my idea that the other man was afraid *we* were the cops!"

Slim asked: "What else, Captain?"

"I want the Siggy Murrah funeral covered. The G-men will be there, too; so be careful. I've got the names of several dentists that I'm going to call on. I'll contact you, Slim, when I'm ready, and give orders for the next meeting."

"Right, Captain. And—" Slim paused. "And The Dutchman and Sol? How about their—?"

Satan stared at the two new members for a long moment. "Give them another try. You must remember, Slim, that things which we encounter and think nothing of are probably horrible experiences for new men." He smiled slightly. "I doubt if any new men ever had to go through what Sol and The Dutchman did to-night."

He paused and gave the two men an encouraging glance.

"Just one warning, though! If I'm right, if this is a jail-break gang and they were watching that cemetery, they must be jittery. And after what happened to-night, they'll be panicky—desperate men to face. Be on your guard, every one of you. Look alive… or you're liable to be looking *very dead* for a long, long time! Good night, men!"

"Night, Cap'n!"

CHAPTER 5
THE DEVIL'S DENTIST

SATAN STOOD across the street from the offices of Anthony Leedrum, dentist. For more than two hours he had stood thus, patiently waiting for the time when Leedrum would be idle, when there would be no patient to take his place in the dentist's chair.

Dressed in a plain black coat and muffler, with a black derby and bone-rimmed spectacles, he was as inoffensive looking as some serious student.

Finally, the chair in that window on the second floor was vacant. Satan waited five minutes more, then crossed the street and mounted the stairs. Inside the offices—there was a small anteroom with the usual magazines and newspapers on a table—he found the dentist alone.

Satan greeted the man, talked casually about some fancied dental work; but he was listening intently for other sounds in that office; wanted to know, before he went into the subject of his mission, if any other person were there. When he was satisfied that the man was alone, he launched into his purpose.

"Doctor," he stated with the utmost casualness, "I had a—er—friend who used to come to you. You did some bridgework for him… a removable bridge. You could identify your work if you saw it?"

Leedrum, a thin, defeated, weary-looking man of middle age, smiled slightly. "I should be able to. In addition, I keep a chart of work I have done. Why?"

Satan came to the point quickly. "Have you a chart for a fellow named Klami?" He watched intently to see what reaction the man would show.

But Leedrum stared blankly back at Satan. "I don't place the name," he confessed. "But wait a moment and I'll look in the files."

Satan waited five minutes, alert for any telephone call the man might try to put in.

When the dentist came back into the anteroom, Satan was reading a magazine.

"Haven't got him," the man confessed. "Can't find a Klami… although the name is vaguely familiar."

"I don't wonder," Satan thought grimly. Aloud, "Well, maybe you can identify these." He produced a packet from his coat and opened it.

The dentist blinked and came forward. His eyes were narrowed when he looked up from his examination of the teeth. "Where did you get these?" he asked coldly.

"Never mind that," Satan told the man, ice in his voice. "I'll do the questioning. Have you ever seen this work before?"

The dentist appraised Satan a long moment, then shrugged. "Come inside," he said briefly, leading the way into his office. Satan followed him cautiously.

The dentist went to a filing cabinet and ruffed quickly through some records there. Finally he stopped, examined one sheet, then drew it out and passed it to Satan. "Here it is. That's the work you have there. But it was done five years ago for a man named Basil Brown."

"Oho!" Satan thought. "Basil Brown, is it? Klami under an alias!" He looked at the chart in his hand; a record of fillings, of extractions, of the making of the bridgework that he had brought with him—all of it, tooth for tooth, on that sheet.

"I guess that's it," he said at last. "Only—how is it you can remember having done that five years ago?"

The man smiled again. "That's easy. Brown's brother was here only—" he paused, calculating—"five months ago, approximately. He asked for a duplication of that work—said Brown had smashed the last one and wanted another like it."

"And you made another set, from this?"

"No. He didn't want that. I made a transcript of the record, as you see it. It puzzled me, because he could have made another set by taking a wax impression of Brown's mouth and doing it without my records."

"I see." Satan considered a moment, then asked slowly,

"Suppose that Brown wasn't—ah—*available,* for that wax impression. Then this record would do?"

"Certainly not. You still need a plate to carry the teeth; the plate must fit the gums. But he wanted it, so I gave it to him."

Satan was more puzzled than ever. "But this set that I have in my hand—this is your work? You're sure of that?"

"Why, of course. I—" The dentist paused, his eyes keened on the things. "Let me have those for a moment!"

Satan watched closely while the little dentist made a minute inspection of the bridgework and the four attached teeth. The man sighed.

"This is Brown's chart, all right," he said at last. "But it isn't my work. Frankly, that is better work than I am capable of. A master workman made these—and he used the finest porcelain that can be bought. My materials are, of necessity, cheap." He indicated his office. "Rich patients don't sit in this chair."

"That's what *you* think!" was Satan's dry comment to himself. But he had the information he wanted. Someone had come before him, had gotten the record of the work done for 'Brown,'—including all the fillings and the various other details of the man's mouth. Enough, at any rate, to *make* another 'Brown' mouth, if it was wanted!

Satan pulled out a wallet and selected a fifty-dollar bill. He stuffed it into the hand of the amazed dentist and walked to the entrance door.

Long before Dr. Leedrum was recovered from his amazement, Satan was on his way to the offices of Dr. Harold Simmiss, in a more fashionable part of town. Simmiss, Doc discovered, had done Joe Mikkle's dental work.

IN THE taxi, Satan spread out the early editions of the afternoon papers. There had been nothing concerning the cemetery incident in the morning papers.

In a small space on one of the inner pages appeared this cryptic bit:

> Vandals violated several plots in nearby Blue Lots Cemetery. No damage was done other than the scarring of several graves, the turf being badly damaged.

Satan frowned. "What the—? No damage done!"

He called to the driver to stop at the corner near the address he was seeking. In a 'phone booth, he called Slim. "Get Soapy over to that cemetery and see what the story is," he ordered tersely. "I want to know why and how this thing was hushed up." He hung up without waiting for an answer.

He raised his brows at the elegance of the apartment house in which the doctor had his offices. They were on the ground floor of a marble palace, and Satan entered the foyer of the building and rang at the bell marked *Dr. Simmiss*.

The door was opened instantly by a girl in a trimly starched, white uniform. Some men in white coats—assistants, Satan judged them to be—were visible through partly-curtained glass doors. A luxurious reception room was to the left, and it was into this room that Satan was ushered.

A door at his right opened and a young woman came out,

pad and pencil poised. Satan looked at her keenly, thought that her eyes were more than a little... afraid.

"Fear," Satan thought. "Or worse. Horror!"

But he dismissed it with a shrug. People had troubles of their own. Still, the girl was undeniably pretty—beautiful, almost; auburn-haired, large brown eyes, clear skin. She attempted a smile and Satan thought he had never seen more perfect teeth.

"About twenty-one," he judged her. "Well, if Joe Mikkle and his kind make use of this dentist, it's no wonder she looks afraid. It's just like Mikkle, this place... the best was never any too good for him. Mikkle probably came here under an alias, too."

He smiled quickly and apologized. "I'm sorry, Miss. I was—er—thinking of something. What did you say?"

"Your name? I don't believe you have an appointment, have you?"

"No, I haven't," Satan confessed. "I came to see the doctor on a matter of importance to me. I thought perhaps he could advise me."

"I'll have to ask him, after I know your business. May I have your name?"

"It isn't important," Satan told her easily. "All I want is some information about making bridgework. What I want to know, is: how nearly can I have a bridgework made to fit a—er—friend, who can't—ah—be seen?"

The girl's eyes widened in astonishment, lost their former fear in a look of sheer wonder. She repeated Satan's question slowly, adding: "Is that right? Is that what you want to know?"

"Right as rain!"

She stood undecided for a moment, then turned and went hesitantly to the door she had come from. Finally she made up her mind, seemingly, and went out, closing the door after her. But before Satan had even settled into one of the luxurious chairs, she was back again.

"The doctor will see you right away," she said, a look of intense curiosity in her eyes.

Satan went through to an inner hall, followed her to the door at the far end. There the girl knocked.

"Come in."

It was a low, clear voice; a voice of utmost dignity and impressiveness; a voice that bespoke the student, the gentleman, the professional man; a voice of gentleness and culture. A truly remarkable voice.

And the man on the other side of the door answered that description in every detail, Satan saw. Tall… as he stood there behind his massive desk in the tastily furnished room… tall, and broad; a man of perhaps fifty years, with a kindly face that was set off by an iron-gray beard. His hair was wavy and thick, his head well-formed.

But what impressed Satan most was the man's eyes. A peculiar shade of blue-gray; almost hypnotic, they were, Satan felt, after a moment's study of them.

Doctor Simmiss moved his hands easily, gracefully. "Won't you sit down, Mr.—?"

"Smith," Satan supplied with a slight smile. "A common name, Doctor. But my mission isn't common."

"Nor is your appearance," the dentist said with a smile, his eyes going meaningly to Satan's close cropped head. But he continued without a pause, "Miss Mellin—won't you come in, Wanda?—Miss Mellin stated your question. I'd like to know more details before I answer."

Satan swung to permit the girl to pass and take a chair. And as he did so, he felt a sudden tenseness in her, saw in her eyes that fearful, almost hunted look which he had noticed when he first came in. He waited until she was seated and then dropped into a chair facing the dentist.

Simmiss took his time in settling himself, however. He stood in silent thought for some minutes, then excused himself and passed through a door at his left. "I'll be right back," he explained with a smile.

While he was gone, Satan took the opportunity of examining the girl again, covertly. She was plainly nervous and agitated. She looked up suddenly, smiled swiftly, fleetingly, then dropped her eyes to her shoe tips again.

Satan stirred, puzzled. "You like your work here?" he asked, making his voice as casual as possible.

"No, I—that is, I mean—" she faltered, looked around quickly. "Yes," she said, finally, in a whisper.

A frown cut twin lines between Satan's eyes. But before he could give the matter any further thought, the dentist was back again.

"Ah, now," the man said, rubbing his hands together, "I am sure you will excuse my absence. A matter of utmost necessity. Now, Mr.—Smith? Is that what you call yourself?"

Satan smiled. "That's it." Briefly, he stated his question.

Simmiss sat and stared at Satan before answering. When he did, his voice was crisp, incisive. "Why can't your friend be seen?"

Satan shrugged, then remembered the man's scrutiny of his close-cropped head. "Perhaps he's in jail?"

Another long scrutiny. Then: "There are dentists in jail. I think we both know that." A pause, and another stare from those hypnotic, green eyes.

"Let's put it this way, Doctor," Satan said outright. "Suppose there is a man in jail whose teeth I wish to duplicate. Duplicate exactly. Is it possible for me to get a record of those teeth, and have a set made like them—to the last detail—so that you can't tell the difference?"

Simmiss' eyes widened slowly until Satan felt as though they were larger than the man's face, even. He had a strange feeling of being drawn toward those eyes, nearer and nearer to them… a feeling that he was going to tumble headlong into them and be engulfed. A strange dryness came into his mouth. He swallowed, tried to look away… couldn't.

All sound seemed stilled and a numbness started at his finger tips and crept up into his shoulders, started up his neck and for his head. Satan put every ounce of power, will power and physical power, into one supreme effort… and moved his body violently.

Dimly, from far away, he heard a yell. He tried to stand, but found that he was on the floor, on all fours. The lights seemed to be coming back into the room, sounds came clear to him. He looked up, saw the girl Wanda Mellin standing close to the wall, terror in her eyes and her hand to her mouth. She was clearly frightened.

Simmiss was sitting at his desk, his piercing eyes staring back into Satan's. "Help him, Wanda," the dentist said in a flat voice. "Mr.—ah—Smith must be ill. I think he had a fainting attack."

Satan waved the girl away, got slowly to his feet. "I—I don't know what happened to me," he said dazedly. "Who—who yelled?"

"You did," Simmiss told him quietly. His voice was cold, inflexible. "Now, sir—let's have an end to this! State your case, clearly and concisely, and I'll do my best to answer you."

"I have stated it," Satan told the man shortly. He felt like a fool, realizing as he did now that Simmiss, whether involuntarily or not, had all but hypnotized him. His eyes went to the girl Wanda, expecting to read derision, contempt. But her eyes looked just as they had before—terrified.

"Your question is absurd," Simmiss told him calmly. "You don't make a man's teeth as you do cigarettes… just roll them and shape them and there they are. Each bridge must be individually fitted. If that's all, Mr.—er—Smith?"

Satan got to his feet and thanked the man coldly. He pulled the wallet from his pocket and looked up.

"How much will that be, Doctor?"

51

"One—thousand—dollars!" the man snapped.

Satan, without batting so much as an eyelash, selected a thousand-dollar bill and casually dropped it on the man's desk. "There you are," he said. "And thank *you*, sir."

But before he turned to go, he had the satisfaction of seeing those eyes bulge… and then narrow to slits.

The door had scarcely shut behind them in the small hall when Wanda Mellin whispered, "I don't know who you are, but I've got to talk with you! I feel that I can trust you, that I—"

The door behind them swung open. "Wanda! I wish to see you. Dr. Costa will show Mr. Smith to the door."

Satan swung around, half-tempted to face Simmiss down, to hear now what it was that Wanda was trying to say. But at the girl's little gesture of surrender, he gave it up.

"This is none of my business," he reasoned. "Anyway, I have more important things to do right now. I can always track back on this thing later."

He turned and made his way to the door. A burly individual in a white coat waited there for him. Satan nodded and stopped. But the assistant motioned toward the door.

"After you, sir."

"Thank you."

Satan started, but he had only taken three steps when a powerful smash behind his left ear brought him to his knees. He struggled to keep his balance, made a grab for the .45 in his arm holster; but he wasn't to make it.

Another stunning blow, and blackness enfolded him.

CHAPTER 6
A PAYOFF IN LEAD

S ATAN REGAINED consciousness with a sense of swinging in a hammock, of being gently see-sawed back and forth. At first, he thought it was a dream… but the twinge of pain that shot through his head when he tried to turn changed his mind on that.

"More like a nightmare than a dream," he muttered. "But what's wrong with me? Why can't I see? What has happened?"

He blinked his eyes against the gray pall that was over them, then tried to sit erect. He was shaken suddenly, roughly.

"Lie still," a voice growled, "or we'll drop you right here and give you some more of the same."

The swinging sensation started again. Satan realized that he was being carried someplace. Another try with his eyes told him that he was tightly blindfolded. He tried to think back, to recollect—

"The cemetery?" he wondered. "No. We finished *that!*" He pondered the puzzle further. "Dr. Leedrum's? No, I left there—"

And then he remembered… the girl, Wanda Mellin… the odd Dr. Harold Simmiss… the burly attendant… and the lights going out.

"So one of Simmiss' assistants floored me, did he?" Satan pondered. "Why? Because I flashed my bankroll?" But immediately he dismissed that. A man who could afford the palatial offices that Simmiss showed would hardly be a footpad.

"He probably confines his robbery to the size of his dental bills," Satan thought.

He lay still, sensed from the pressure on his back and sides that he was on a stretcher. But where? His bearers had been walking long enough since his consciousness to have covered that entire apartment three times, Satan realized. "And why the blindfold?"

At a sudden thought, he exerted pressure with his left arm against his side. A warm glow flowed over his body when he felt the lump that told him his gun hadn't been discovered… hadn't been removed, at any rate.

And then, with a definite bump, he was lowered to the floor.

"Lock the door and let him up," he heard a cold, hard voice… a voice that he recognized to be that of Simmiss.

A rough hand tore the bandage from Satan's eyes. Another pair of hands jerked him to a sitting position, then to his feet. Satan staggered weakly a moment, shielding his eyes from the sudden light with a forearm. His arm was brutally struck down. "Keep your hands still," he was told in a savage growl.

"Nice guys," Satan tried to kid. "Just what's the big idea?"

A stinging smash in the mouth brought hot blood to his lips. Satan clenched his hands and checked his slowly rising gorge. Better to have some idea what he was up against—the odds against him—before he tried any rough stuff.

He opened his eyes, peered through them at the dim figures in the room—Simmiss… the big attendant who had struck him down… and another man, also a husky bruiser. Satan let his eyes rove over the place. He saw from the stone walls, from the steel-shuttered window and the door at one end, that he was in a cellar of some sort.

Satan wanted to see down at the other end of the room. He made as if to stagger from weakness, turned a half circle, stopped. At the other end of the room was a brightly lighted corner, fitted out like an operating room. The high, white table… the strong lights that were suspended above it… the cabinet with instruments. Satan puzzled, but he was too canny to stare at it long. He turned to confront Dr. Simmiss.

The man was staring again, staring with those widening eyes that'd had such a peculiar, hypnotic effect on Satan but a short time before. This time, however, Satan managed a slight laugh.

"Lay off that stuff, Doc. You nearly had me in your office… but I'm wise to you now. Just what is your game?"

"Lissen," the burly thug growled, "cut it or I'll give you more of what you got upstairs!"

Upstairs! Satan fought down the feeling of triumph. So this den… whatever it was… was directly below Dr. Simmiss' office! At any rate, Satan knew where he was, now.

"Shut up, Costa," Simmiss snapped. "What have I told you about shooting your mouth off?"

Satan saw his chance and drove another wedge of conversation in. "I don't know what this is all about," he said, "but if it's robbery, I wish you'd get it over with and let me out of here."

And then came the shock of the thing—of his position—in full force.

"We are not robbers," Simmiss said slowly and meaningly.

55

"It is not our game to steal from people. But, my friend, you never shall leave here… *alive!*"

FOR A brief moment, Satan was minded to go after his gun, to shoot it out with these men, whoever they were and whatever their purpose was. But he fought for a cool head.

He slid his eyes around… saw that the man called Costa had a small, flat automatic of some foreign make in his left hand. That was that!

Satan's estimate of these men changed in a flash. He had thought them robbers; and maybe they were. But on Simmiss' own words, they were murderers as well!

Coolly, Satan stood his ground and waited for the next move. After a long pause, Simmiss asked in what was almost a whisper: "Who *are* you?"

"I told you," Satan said easily. "My name is Smith."

"You're a Federal man!" Simmiss snapped.

A bomb exploded in Satan's brain. So Simmiss was afraid of the Feds! And suspected that he, Satan, was one of them! Why? Because he had come in with a full wallet? That was ridiculous? Because… *because…*

"Because I came with that question about teeth?" Satan wondered. "But why should that get him suspicious, unless there was some reason why Simmiss feared that question?" The memory of the fear in Wanda Mellin's eyes came back to him.

Much as he hated to suspect her, Satan couldn't help but notice the similarity in the fear that she had shown and in the fear that Simmiss now showed. But she had been trying to tell him something when—

"Search him," came Simmiss' harsh order, breaking in on his thoughts.

Costa and the other man patted Satan's coat expertly. Costa thrust his hand inside Satan's coat and came out with the automatic. But there was nothing else to be found, other than the wallet. Satan never carried identification of any kind with him.

Just the automatic, Satan's gold cigarette case, and his automatic lighter, were brought forth. He had left the Klami teeth at Leedrum's.

"So!" Simmiss breathed. "You go armed, my friend, when you call on dentists!" He took the gun and examined it for a number; and his eyes narrowed when he saw that they had been filed away.

"I seem to need a gun when I call on dentists like you," Satan told him drily.

But Simmiss was staring at him intently, not even hearing him. "And why are the numbers filed away, my friend?"

Satan was silent a moment; then shrugged. "There's only one answer to that," he said in the manner of making a confession. "The gun is... stolen. It was a police gun."

He saw Simmiss and the other two exchange glances. Then Costa spoke.

"How about testing him out, Chief? He looks and acts like a tough cookie. I hit him hard enough upstairs to kill an ox—and still he tried to go for his gat."

Satan's eyes widened. But he stood silent, his mind racing with the thing. "Test me out for what? Why? What's this all about?" he wondered.

But Simmiss cut in. "That's out. This man *knows* something, and if he didn't know *before* he was here, he does now. No, Costa. *He goes!*"

Satan's blood ran cold at Costa's next question. The burly thug had picked up Satan's automatic lighter and was examining the thing closely. "Chief," he said, his eyes shining, "can I have this thing? Gee, it's a pip!"

"Dividing my things before I'm even killed!" Satan marvelled. "This is a nice bunch!"

Simmiss ignored the man.

"**THE LIGHTS,**" he said, looking at the other man in the room. "Turn off the lights in here. Just leave that small one over there by the table." As the man spoke, he drew an automatic from his own pocket. "We'll use chloroform. It isn't so messy that way."

Satan watched from the corner of his eye while the other assistant snapped the light switch in the place, throwing the whole lower end of the room in darkness. Only a small light burned in that operating alcove.

Simmiss took a step in Satan's direction, while the man Costa stood and toyed with the lighter, snapping its flame on and off. The man seemed intrigued with it.

Costa had discovered the small hidden button in the side of it—a button that connected with a battery in the lower half of the gadget. It was half lighter and half flashlight. Satan tensed himself, a wild hope springing up in his heart. He had been on the point of hurling himself at the dentist—suicide, almost, with a man of that type, Satan knew. But now he tensed, his muscles set and his eyes glued on Costa.

"What's this button do?" the man was murmuring. "Do you use this when you're filling it, or—" He pressed on the button.

Instantly, a weird light sprang into being on that steel door at the darkened end of the room. Costa didn't see it right away, engrossed as he was with the new plaything. But Simmiss seemed to sense something. He couldn't see it from his present position, but he stopped. The other assistant was unlocking a door near that operating table. It looked like a closet door.

"The supply closet, where they keep the chloroform," Satan guessed.

And then Simmiss turned and saw for the first time that weird light that was on the door; that light which came from the bottom of the cigarette lighter that Costa was playing with; a light that was loosed when the big thug pressed that hidden button on the side of the lighter.

And in the center of that light, looming large against the steel panel of the door… *was the figure of Satan with his pitchfork raised to the attack!*

The effect of the thing on Simmiss was instantaneous and devastating. By chance, Costa was holding the lighter so that the Satanic figure was almost the exact height of the door—was so arranged on the door that it seemed as if the frightening apparition was leaping in on them.

Simmiss stumbled, croaked for one brief second, then loosed an ear-piercing shriek.

"Satan! Satan! My God, it's Captain Satan!"

He ripped a withering burst of fire from his automatic at the thing, was joined in a split second by the assistant who had been at the back of the room. Costa stood rooted to his spot, his eyes bulging and his hand clamped in a death grip on the lighter.

Satan saw his chance… and acted.

With the speed of a trained fighter, he threw his weight into a crushing punch that took Simmiss' helper flush on the side of the jaw. At the same time his other hand flashed out and wrenched the gun loose from the man's already nerveless grip.

Simmiss heard… turned. But Satan fired from the hip with his left hand. The bullet—a .38—blasted Simmiss around, slammed him up against the wall. But he came back fighting; shooting. One shot creased Satan's shoulder. Another dusted his cheek with hot air.

Satan fired again. Simmiss stumbled, clutched at his gun arm, sank to his knees with a groan. But Costa had come out of his trance, had dropped the lighter, was bringing his own gun into play. A surge of savageness swept over Satan.

This was the gang that had slugged him! This was the gang that had trapped him in a cellar, was going to chloroform him, like a dog! This was the gang that would divvy up a victim's goods even before they had murdered him.

Two snap-shots smashed the gun from Costa's hand, even as another drilled a hole into the man's forehead. Costa went down without having fired so much as one shot.

Working fast, his brain still seething, Satan stepped to the light switch and snapped it on. The other assistant was still unconscious. First, Satan retrieved his lighter, then took the guns from the dead Costa and the unconscious dentist. The second assistant's gun went, also. After pocketing his wallet, Satan remembered the thousand dollar fee he had paid to Simmiss in the office.

He dropped the three captured guns into a pocket, held his own at ready until he had searched the dentist. In an inside pocket he found a fat money carrier. A glance brought a gasp to his lips.

"It's *all* mine," Satan gritted. "That's my fee—'Doctor' Satan's fee!" He grabbed a pencil and notebook from Simmiss' pocket and made a hasty scrawl on one of the pages… the Satanic figure with pitchfork upraised.

"And there's my receipt!" he said, as he stepped for the door.

He heard footsteps on the stairs outside, wrenched the door open and fired a burst straight ahead. The steps scrambled back and out of hearing. Satan peered, saw a door to the right. He jumped to it. It gave onto an alley.

With the speed of a sprinter, Satan covered the distance to a right turn, saw a ramp that led to another door. He slid along it, holding close to the wall. It let onto the street.

Satan turned down the avenue at the end of the street and hurried on for several blocks. Then he stopped, slipped into a doorway, watched back on his track to see if he was being followed.

Ten minutes later, he stepped into a telephone booth and called Slim.

"Get four of our best men—our best scrappers," he ordered

tersely. "I've come across something that I want to investigate further. I'm not a suspicious man by nature, Slim—but unless I'm crazy, I think I've just been interviewing a very big and very dangerous crook! If I'm not mistaken, Slim, it's *the* crook!"

CHAPTER 7
SIN, INCORPORATED

IT WAS two in the morning when the sleek limousine made its tenth slow circle of the block where Dr. Simmiss' offices were located. And the place had been under watch of one of Satan's men for a number of hours previous.

Now the car slowed and Pat stepped out of the shadows.

"Sure you saw no lights? Nothing?"

"Nothing, Cap'n," the watch reported. "Place is quiet as a churchyard."

Satan chuckled. "It's good you didn't say 'graveyard,' Pat!" He thought for a moment. "Get over to that service entrance door and see if it's open. If it isn't—"

"It'll be open if you want it that way, Cap'n," Pat said mildly.

The car circled again, stopped near the corner of the avenue. Satan, Slim and Gentleman Dan climbed down. "Set the car down in a nearby garage and hustle back here," Satan told Kayo. "We'll wait in the service alley. You saw the door?"

"Right, Cap'n."

The car slid away and up the street. The leader of the crew and his two men walked rapidly up the Avenue. As they came alongside the service door to the apartment house, it swung open slightly. "In here, Cap'n," Pat called in a sibilant whisper.

A split second later the street was deserted again… except for the uniformed patrolman who swung around the corner and walked slowly along his beat.

Within five minutes, Kayo had joined the four who huddled in that alley. "A harness bull just made his tour," he whispered.

Satan nodded. "Heard him going by. He tried this door to see if it was locked. It's good we had slipped the catch back on as a precaution. Let's go!"

Silently, the five men went down the ramped incline, silently tried the second door. It was locked. Pat tried a number of keys, finally gave it up and worked the lock with a piece of wire.

They found the inner door—the entrance to the 'operating room' and the scene of Satan's battle with Simmiss— open. Satan motioned the others to drop back out of ear range.

"This is funny," he whispered. "The door is wide open… and there hasn't been a light in front all night. What do you make of it?"

"They're waiting for us," Gentleman Dan said. "They expect we're coming back."

Slim shook his head. "I think the Captain stumbled onto something real, when he walked in on this Simmiss. Remember, the mob behind this jail-cracking scheme has to have a dentist, if the Captain's theory is right. Maybe this is the lad!"

"That's my guess, of course," Satan admitted. "Maybe they're loaded for bear and waiting for us."

"Aw," Kayo growled, "they were scared to death when they

saw that silhouette-lamp, on the bottom of your lighter, pop up on that door. They're probably running yet—those that are alive."

"Sure, that's my notion, too, Cap'n," Pat put in. "But one way or another, let's go in and find out. The five of us can take fifteen of the likes of them any day in the week!"

Satan chuckled. "It's good we're not all Irish, Pat. I don't think the crew would last a week!" But Pat's suggestion carried.

"I'm for Pat's idea," Slim admitted. "Let's see what's in this thing, now. Anyway, I'd like to get a crack at that mob—trying to chloroform you!"

Satan's face was grim when he gave the signal. Stealthily, the five men went through the door. Satan stopped Pat with his hand and pointed to the stairs that led to a rear door in the Simmiss apartment. "Stand guard here. We don't want to be trapped. If that door opens even a crack—let 'em have it!"

Satan unlimbered his lamp from his coat pocket, flashed it briefly on the steel door that let into the room where he'd had such a narrow escape. "Get your guns set, men," he whispered. "I'll try the door gently. It's probably locked. But if it isn't, I'll blaze the light and we'll rush the place. Try to get them alive, if you can. But if they open up on us, show them no mercy!"

Slim, Kayo and Gentleman Dan crouched low, their eyes glued to the door they could just see in front of them. Standing as flat as he could get against the wall, Satan put out a hand and pushed gently at the door.

He took a step, pushed again before he realized that the door was coming slowly open. With a clucked warning to his men, he gently applied more and more pressure. The door was swinging wide on oiled hinges, soundlessly, effortlessly.

"Now!" Satan barked, snapping his lamp into a blazing light. His men jumped forward, their guns trained on…

A white, stone-walled room, spotlessly clean!

THE FIVE men stood in silent wonder. Instead of a shambles, instead of the scene of a knock-down drag-out fight, they were in a room that was bare and white as a winter field.

"Well, I'll be—" Satan murmured.

"Sure you got the right place, Captain?" Slim asked.

Pat was staring critically at the walls. "I'll say he has. Look at the bullet marks on the wall over here!"

Silently, the crew inspected the place. The supply closet at the rear was empty. But the operating table stood where it had been when Satan had seen it. Gentleman Dan examined the floor. "Been washed in the last few hours," he reported. "I can smell the cleaning stuff."

"It looks as though they've skipped," Satan admitted. "But it may be just a trap. We'll tackle the upstairs part, now."

They made their way cautiously up the stone stairs. The shades of the place were drawn; but that door, too, was unlocked. Satan flashed his lamp for the second time. And for the second time his backers charged an empty stronghold.

The upper part of the offices was as spotless as the operating room. But it wasn't bare. Chairs, tables, rugs, office equipment, cases of dental instruments, drills, X-ray machines, drawers of materials for the treatment and filling and cleaning of teeth— all stood in perfect order.

But the files were empty, and there was not so much as a single patient's card in the place. They went through the apartment, turning on the lights.

Hot slugs whined from back
of the headstone.

"It's a nice layout," Gentleman Dan observed. "*Very* nice. Not only an office, but a home as well. Take a look down here."

A hall to the left opened on five bedrooms and three baths, a kitchen, butler's pantry, and a private sitting room fitted out as a library.

"The mob stayed right here," Slim observed. "Beds made, dishes washed, plenty of food in the place. Not bad at all. In fact, a very nice place."

"Hey," Gentleman Dan called out, a worried frown creasing his brow. "Has it occurred to you that this dentist may be the real thing? He may be nothing but that, and you've scared the living lights out of him?"

"Now, Dan," Satan chaffed him. "How many plain, ordinary, decent dentists conk their patients and offer to rub them out with chloroform?"

"That's right," Gentleman Dan admitted. "But the place certainly looks on the up-and-up. It's got me."

"A front," Slim suggested. "The best place to hide is out in the open. Then nobody will suspect you of hiding. Take it from me, no honest crew—no matter how crazy—will run because someone fights back at them when they jump him. If these people are honest, they're lunatics. And we know they're not lunatics."

Satan nodded. "Slim's right. This is a wrong bunch. And it's a wrong bunch with a right racket. Twenty thousand dollars was the sum of money that I took from—er—that my friend Simmis paid me for my professional services today. That's a bit more than cigarette money."

"Ah—" Gentlemen Dan began. But he stopped.

Satan smiled. "Yes, Dan! The usual split prevails!"

Gentleman Dan grinned at the general laugh that went up at his expense. "Can't blame a guy for trying," he said. "I was just—"

He stopped. A telephone was ringing in one of the other rooms.

Kayo spoke up. "Now ain't that sumpin! Whose move is it now?"

The five stood silent, Satan pondering, the other four watching their leader intently. At last he moved, raising his hands in a gesture of resignation.

"That, gentlemen, is one of the penalties of housebreaking. The least we can do is to answer the man's 'phone for him." He led the way to the room where the telephone was ringing in a modulated but persistent tone.

But he changed his mind suddenly and motioned to Gentleman Dan to take it. "This bunch knows my voice, Dan. You take it. Talk just as though you belong here all the time. There's a chance—just a chance, mind you—that it *may* be something important."

Gentleman Dan nodded and picked up the receiver.

"Doctor Simmiss' office," he said in the most modulated and cultured of voices. "May I be of service to you?"

AFTER LISTENING for a moment, Gentleman Dan's face broke into the broadest of smiles. He said, "Just a moment" and turned to Satan and the other three.

"There is a gentleman by the name of Davies Duggan on the

telephone. He announces that he has what he believes to be an impacted wisdom tooth, and wishes an appointment with Dr. Simmiss. The tooth is giving him hell and he can't sleep."

Kayo guffawed. But Satan silenced him with a look. "Maybe it's a code," he pointed out. "Maybe this is one of the things that we want to get next to. Tell him to come over at—" he considered—"ten o'clock in the morning."

"Yeah," Pat grinned. "And ask him hasn't he got any consideration? The idea of waking people like us up at this time of the morning!"

Gentleman Dan delivered Satan's instructions and listened to what the man on the other end had to say. Finally: "No; you can't come earlier. Doctor has had a very busy schedule and may not be able to see you at all. But we'll take care of you some way—Mr. Duggan. *Good* night!"

"Now what?" Slim asked.

"We sleep here," Satan decreed. "And in the morning, we line up to receive our visitor all dressed in those nice white coats we saw in that store room back yonder."

"Set a guard?"

"Don't need it. These fellows have run out of it, whatever it is. Slim, you go out and call the rest of the boys. Tell them to be on deck here by nine in the morning. The whole crowd. Better start them at eight, and space them ten minutes apart."

"Can't I call from here, Captain?"

Satan's voice was icy. "Our telephone numbers, Slim, are as sacred as our identities. We have to show our faces to one another, but what our real names and our real identities are

70

shall be known *only* to you and to me. Besides, we don't want any calls traced from this number."

"Sorry, Captain. I forgot. But—" He paused. "That brings up a question. Do we want to trust The Dutchman and Sol this early in their trial?"

"You brought them in, Slim. Don't you trust them?"

"Sure I do, Captain. But that show they put up at the cemetery the other night? That was pretty bad."

Satan smiled slightly. "To tell you the truth. Slim—I don't blame them a bit. They've had time to get over their shakes by now, and probably will prove to be valuable men. We need them, so bring them along, too."

Slim started for the door, but Satan shot him a warning. "There'll be a doorman or two on duty out there. Tell them you haven't your key and will want to get back in again."

Slim nodded and was gone.

And the telephone rang again.

"Business is picking up," Gentleman Dan murmured as he picked up the receiver for the second time. "Hello?" he said into the instrument.

Satan stepped close when he saw him stiffen. Gentleman Dan held the 'phone so that Satan could hear, too. It was a husky, low voice that came from the other end.

"Dis is Benny de Fog," the voice said. "I got a job f'r de chief." Satan took the instrument.

"What's the idea of calling at this time of night?" he barked.

"Chees, Chief," the voice of Benny the Fog apologized. "De

guy has got to be sprung day after tomorrow! How can I help it?"

Satan's face lighted up and his gray eyes glistened. "You did perfectly right, Benny. See me at eleven tomorrow. Oh—I forgot to say that I have some new—er—boys on the job. They're O.K. to talk to in case I'm tied up."

"Lissen, Chief," Benny the Fog pleaded. "I don't wanna see nobody but you! I'll show whenever you say. An' I use the servants' entrance, huh?"

"You heard what I said," Satan said severely.

"You're de tops," Benny the Fog gave in. "I'll show at eleven."

Satan turned to the others in triumph. "A sweet soul by the name of Benny the Fog is coming to discuss a 'springing.' At eleven. I seem to have struck it rich, boys!"

Kayo pondered. "But how about the guy with the implanted wisdom tooth?"

"Impacted," Gentleman Dan corrected him. "What about him? He's coming at ten."

"Then," Kayo persisted, "that guy is on the level. He *has* got a bad tooth! What are we going to do with him?"

"It's code, it's code," Pat argued. "When he says he wants a tooth out, it means that he has a customer to be sprung."

"It's all right by me," Kayo gave it up.

Slim came back and Satan reported the conversation. The lieutenant stood in silent thought for some minutes, then shook his head. "The water is getting very deep, Captain. Are you sure you're ready for what this implies? This is a very tough game you're bucking!"

"Tough on the United States if I *don't* buck it," Satan reminded him.

Slim shrugged. "I'll follow wherever you lead. But it looks bad!"

Satan thought for a moment, then smiled slowly. "Boys," he announced. "We're going into a new business, it seems—a business of taking contracts to free criminals so they may sin again—free them at a profit! Our new name?... *'Sin, Incorporated!'*"

But the eyes of both Satan and Slim were sober when they met.

CHAPTER 8
GUN GAMBLER

SATAN SLEPT but a few hours that night. With Slim, he went over the details of the next morning's action; which of the men would be in office uniform; where the others would be quartered; the covering of developments in the Murnell murder; and the Siggy Murrah funeral.

By eight, Slim and Pat were attired in natty white coats. Satan wore his usually severe black suit and bone-rimmed glasses. Gentleman Dan refreshed his memory on the duties of a personal secretary. Kayo, in his chauffeur's garb, was both useful and little in evidence. He dusted the offices thoroughly and then repaired to the room below stairs to maintain a watch on that part of the plant.

By nine, Soapy, Doc, Big Bill, Sol and The Dutchman had

been ushered into the new headquarters. The Dutchman, after listening to the news, went through the offices clucking with delight at the various bits of equipment that he saw, examined the supply drawers and cabinets with a loving eye.

Soapy had reported that the supposed burial place of Joe Mikkle, in the suburbs of Philadelphia, was under close and secret scrutiny; and that the watchmen at Blue Lots Cemetery had—with the aid of some heavy 'sugar money'—revealed that the Klami incident at the grave had been merely a little matter, of gang revenge. No investigation had been made by the police; none was wanted by the cemetery officials.

"So the lads who buried that dummy *know* we weren't G-men," Satan pointed out to Slim. "But *how* do they know it?"

"That's easy," Slim answered. "G-men aren't in the habit of running out on a lone gunman, or even a hundred gunmen. And they would have fixed things with the cemetery people and done the digging properly and secretly."

"Check." Satan thought for a moment. "Let that part of it cook a while."

Sol was assigned for later duty on the Murrah funeral and burial. Soapy was detailed to the job of door-opener. Doc was to trace the permits for chloroform which Simmiss must have had. Big Bill was put on guard at the service entrance, with orders to follow directly in back of anyone strange who came into the place.

And at ten minutes past nine, the landlord's representative came.

"Dr. Simmiss isn't here," Gentleman Dan told him coolly. "Anything I can do?"

"You and the rest of you can get out," the man said shortly. He was a short, stout, bustling man with an air of great authority and the broadest black ribbon on his glasses that Gentleman Dan had ever seen. And the thickest lenses in those glasses, as well.

Slim took charge. "We're very busy," he said genially. "Come back next week, won't you?"

"You won't be here next week!" The man fished a paper from his wallet. "There was some sort of disturbance here last night. Shots were heard, I am told."

"Some ether exploded."

"What? Where?"

"In the store room downstairs. No damage done." Slim stuffed the paper into the man's vest. "You'd better keep this."

The little man bristled. "Here, here! What are you—?"

Slim bent and picked something from the floor. "Is this your wallet? The papers seem to be falling out of it." He handed it to the agent. "Bless my soul! This can't be your watch? Over here on the desk? Very careless, sir; *very* careless!"

The little man removed his glasses and peered. "What the—? How did that get there?"

Slim shrugged and began to pare his nails with a pen-knife. "I'm sure I can't tell you." He passed close to the man and stopped a few steps away. The agent peered at the watch, restored it to his pocket and fumbled for his glasses.

"Looking for something?"

"My—my glasses. Where are they? I can't see a foot ahead of me without them!"

"They were moored to you by a hawser, weren't they?" Slim asked.

The agent muttered and fumbled and peered, his lids narrowed to mere peeps. Slim took him by the elbow. "Better go home and sleep it off, old man," he said. "Don't you say anything about this visit, and we won't. That all right?"

He propelled the man to the door and called one of the hall men. "Give this little chap a hand," he said, solicitously. "And not a word to the boss about it!"

Gentleman Dan shook his head when Slim came back in. "Good going, Slim. But hadn't you better give the lad back his glasses?"

"I slipped them into his right hand pocket as he went out," Slim said.

And then the door buzzer sounded.

"Under cover, all of you, excepting Slim and Pat," Satan snapped. "It's ten o'clock—and that'll be Mr. Davies Duggan with his alleged impacted tooth!" He paused, frowning. "Benny the Fog comes through the service entrance, and this man in the front door. I wonder why?"

"He's a big shot," Pat guessed.

"I'll listen from the next room," Satan decided. The buzzer sounded again. "Let Pat handle it, Slim. I don't want you to be spotted unless it's absolutely necessary, or until we know what this fellow's game is."

Davies Duggan came in, his eyes dull and one hand to his jaw.

"What do you want?" Pat asked truculently.

Davies Duggan held his jaw from popping too wide in astonishment. "Wha—what do I want?" he managed. "What do you think I want? I want something pulled, naturally! Oh, oh, oh!"

Pat wasn't impressed. "Don't you mean, *sprung?*"

Duggan stared. "Is that the way you do it now?"

"Now and again! For dough on the line!"

Satan, listening from the other side of the door, went swiftly to the room where his men were waiting. "Gentleman Dan! Get out there and ease Pat out of that! You—Dutchman! How much dentistry do you know?"

The Dutchman smiled. "Try me."

"Okay! Snap into a white coat, man one of those chairs, and look that fellow over. Simmiss, unfortunately, seems to have some regular practice."

The truculent Pat was relegated below stairs and Davies Duggan was installed in a chair. The Dutchman neatly and painlessly extracted an abscessed molar, and the decks were cleared for the visit of Benny the Fog.

Satan ordered: "Keep under cover, all of you; excepting Soapy. I want you to be set, *in uniform,* in case this man tries to back out when he finds a different crowd here. Make it snappy!"

At eleven sharp, Kayo called through the speaking tube that connected with downstairs: "Solo guy coming down the alley!

Tried to turn back when he saw Big Bill behind him, but the Big Fellow gave him the office to keep coming."

"Let him come!" Satan said tensely.

BENNY THE FOG was a narrow-shouldered, thin man, rather short, with the pinched face and nervous manner of a dope addict. He came slowly up the rear stairs, stopping to snatch several looks over his shoulder at the burly figure of Big Bill.

Soapy let him in. "Hi-ya, mug!"

Benny the Fog stared, his eyes suddenly stilled. "I know you. I seen you before. But not here."

"Cut the chin music and ankle in," Soapy said. "This way." He led the way through the back room, into the small hall that connected with Simmiss' office, rapped on the door.

"Come in," Satan called in a curt voice.

Soapy pushed the door open and said, "Step lively: Don't crowd!"

But Benny the Fog stood rooted in his tracks, his eyes wary. He stared at Satan a moment, took in the close-cropped head, the severe black-rimmed glasses, black silk shirt and tie, black suit. Then his eyes slid right and left, as if looking for an escape. He seemed to abandon the thought and his eyes came back to Satan.

"What's de game?" he whispered. "Dere's something phony here!"

"Come in," Satan said quietly. "Come in before you're dragged in, Benny!"

Benny the Fog went in. Soapy pulled the door shut and left

the two of them alone. But the little underworld man didn't sit down. He backed up against the door and stood, his eyes riveted to Satan's gray ones.

"If it ain't a phony, where's the Chief? And the dame—the new dame?"

"They're not here." Satan's voice was curt. "Get down to business."

Benny the Fog smiled. "No! Not me. I ain't crackin' a thing till I see de Chief."

Satan pressed a button and Soapy opened the door. Before he could address a word to the leader, Satan cut him short. "Bring in the boys!" He shifted his eyes to Benny the Fog. The man licked his lips nervously but stood where the opened door had pushed him… midway into the room. But his chin trembled when he heard the steady tramp of men coming down the hall.

Satan's Crew filed solemnly and terrifyingly into the room, shrouded in black capes, their eyes stabbing at Benny the Fog through the slits in their masks as they passed him. With steady tread they trooped along the wall behind Satan's chair and lined up in a semi-circle, their eyes riveted to the stranger.

Satan sat motionless, his mind attacking the problem from every angle. At length, he spoke:

"Going to talk, Benny?"

"Nuh. I don't know nothin'. Yuh can't scare me, fella."

"No?" Satan's cold smile overspread his features. He reached under the table and got his big lamp, laid it flat on the glass desk top, signaled Slim to snap off the room lights.

Benny the Fog made a break for the door but was stopped—and not by any physical force.

An eerie light sprang alive in the room, a light that seemed to come from the ceiling of the place, a yellowish-green light that was split in the center with the Satanic figure floating seemingly in midair, the raised pitchfork threatening Benny the Fog. But Benny didn't see it for a moment....

He was staring wide-eyed at the masked faces that seemed to float in the room, that grew out of the darkness and glared at him through that yellow and green haze. And then his eyes went to the ceiling.

He gasped and clutched at his throat. His mouth sagged wide and he staggered, crashed back against the door. He hid his eyes in the crook of his elbow, shook his head dazedly, then slowly looked up over his shoulder again at that figure floating in the air near the ceiling.

"Satan!" he moaned. "Oh, my God, it's Satan! Captain Satan!"

Satan had shed his bone glasses and had slipped on a mask. "I'm Captain Satan," he said in a hollow, chilling voice.

Benny the Fog was on his knees, his mouth contorted and his eyes mad with fright. "Satan!" he whispered, still clutching at his throat. "I—I always claimed you wuz a fake, a phony! I—I didn't believe you wuz real!"

Benny the Fog collapsed on the floor, sobbing and writhing. It was the only sound in the room for several minutes. Then the silence was broken by that hollow, dead voice again.

"Rise—Benny the Fog! Rise and speak to me now."

Benny the Fog lay as he was for a moment, then raised his

PAROLE FOR THE DEAD

Joe Desher

Kayo

Dutch

eyes fearfully. He moaned anew, came to all fours, gripped the desk and struggled to his feet. "I'll talk!" he sobbed. "I'll talk! I'll spill de whole thing, only—turn on de lights!"

"Talk now! Or be silent forever more! Talk, Benny the Fog! You haven't long to live unless you do!"

Benny the Fog clutched the desk for support, made an attempt to raise his eyes, gave it up. His head down, eyes closed, his teeth chattering with fright, he whispered:

"What do you want to know?"

SATAN SAT silent a long moment. Then: "Who is it you want sprung? From where? Whose order is it?"

"Nicky Carfano," was the whispered answer. "From de Toombs. It come straight from Nick."

"The blackmailer?" Satan thought a moment. "It's got to be done tomorrow?"

"Yeah. Dey wouldn't admit him to no bail."

"You've had contact with Simmiss before? What is his real name?"

There was no answer for a moment. Then: "I dunno."

Satan was calm, inexorable, but deadly. "You've had contact with Simmiss before? What is his real name?"

Benny the Fog surrendered. "Yeh, I seen him, plenty often. I'm de go-between for him and four mobs. I don't know what his name is if it ain't Simmiss."

"Where did you first meet him? Through whom?"

"He was Joe Mikkle's dentist. Dat's all I know. I used to be pay-off man for Mikkle."

"Where is Mikkle now?"

Silence. And then, "He's—dead. Stony."

"Where is Mikkle now? That thing in the grave isn't Mikkle!"

Benny the Fog gestured hopelessly and wiped his nose with the back of his hand. "He's—in Mexico."

Satan smiled, a slow smile that started at the corners of his mouth. The air of the room was stirred by the sighs of relief that came from some of the crew members.

"I was right!" Satan whispered. *"I was right!"* He didn't remove his mask, but he said, "Slim! Snap on the lights! Give Benny the Fog a chair. I think he and I can get together now."

The terrified go-between expelled a whistling sigh of relief and fell into the chair that Slim pushed over to him. "I'm in de bag now," he said weakly. "You an' Simmiss got me between yuh. But I'll string with you."

"That's sensible," Satan said mildly. He toyed with the fountain pen on the desk a moment, then pushed it from him. "You see, Benny, I'll show you just how the thing stands. Simmiss has been in this jail break business and doing very well at it. Right? Well, the situation is just this: I've muscled in on him. *I'm making a bid for that business!"*

CHAPTER 9
SUICIDE SNATCH

SATAN DISMISSED the crew, with the exception of Slim. Benny the Fog looked his relief when the masked men filed out.

"Speak fast," Satan said, after the door had closed. "What's in this job—the Carfano break?"

"Fifty grand—if he's sprung with a stiff to take his place and clear him permanent. Half of dat if it's just a run-out powder."

Satan pondered. Fifty thousand—if Carfano could be made to look dead, could be wiped from the record? Didn't sound like enough for a man of Carfano's wealth, especially in view of the lengthy jail term he was facing.

"You're a liar," he told Benny the Fog.

The man cringed. "I mean, dat much down. De other half on delivery."

"Who provides the corpse?" Slim asked.

Benny stared. "You guys, naturally! I got de dope here." He pulled some papers from his pocket. "Size—weight—what he's wearing—an' de dope on his snappers."

"Snappers?" Satan stared at Slim. "He means teeth. Do you see, Slim? Every time, for this thing to be foolproof, fingerprints must be destroyed... and the identification made by the teeth."

Benny the Fog sat up. "Hey! If you guys are amachoors—"

"Shut up," Satan told him. He turned back to Slim. "A prison riot could shake him clear; but others would be hurt, killed, maybe. We've got to engineer this thing so we get Carfano out with as little fireworks as possible."

Slim shook his head sorrowfully. "I'm against it." But he quieted at Satan's look.

Satan was silent for a moment. Then: "Get Doc and The Dutchman in here." When the two had reported, "Doc? Here's the description of a man." He handed him a piece of paper.

"Can you, from your hospital contacts or elsewhere, get a corpse that could pass for the man described—*providing it had been in a fire before it was found?*"

Doc licked his lips. "I think so," he said quietly. But his eyes were averted.

Satan said softly, "Doc, I don't like it either. But what counts is the big game behind it—what we're trying to do. There's no other way." He turned to The Dutchman.

"Here's a chart of dental work. Could you duplicate this… on that corpse?"

The Dutchman paled. But he kept his voice even. "I can, Cap'n."

"How soon can you get the body?" Satan asked Doc.

The medical member of the crew shrugged. "A day or two."

"No go. It's got to be done to-day."

Doc nodded. "Let me have that paper, Cap'n. I'd better get started." He took the specifications and left. Satan turned to The Dutchman. "Get your things ready to work. Will it be a hard job?"

The Dutchman shook his head. "Maybe I'll have to build the whole mouth over. I won't know until I see… *it*."

Satan dismissed him and turned back to Benny the Fog. "I'm going to let you go, for the time being." He saw the relief in the man's eyes, and smiled. "But first you'll leave that money with me. Then I know you'll be back, and that you won't do anything rash."

The Fog sighed and produced an envelope that was bulging with currency.

Satan counted the bills and nodded. "All in order, Benny. Now you jam out of here, get back into your mobs, and spread this message: *Tell them that Captain Satan has muscled in on the jail break racket and is the man to see from now on!*"

Before Benny left, Satan warned him, "If you let *anyone* know where I am—your number is up!"

The go-between shivered at the look in those gray eyes. But before he went, he had five hundred dollars, that Satan had given him, in his hand.

"Chees, Captain Satan," he whined, "I won't do nothin' to spoil dis racket! I never got nothin' like dis before."

Satan said: "There's twice that waiting for you when you let me know where Simmiss is to be found! That's all. Call me to-night at eleven, and I'll let you know the details."

After the man had gone, Slim shook his head. "I don't get you. Captain. You really mean you're going to spring Carfano?"

Satan showed his impatience. "Slim, do I know where Simmiss is? No! Then how do I get him? I muscle in on his racket and *bring him to me!* Get it?"

Light dawned in Slim's eyes. "*I* see. And then?"

"And then I clean Simmiss and wrap him up for delivery to the G-men. But there's one thing bothering me. That girl—the kid that Simmiss had working for him. I can't figure her in this racket, and I'm afraid for her. She wouldn't have much of an alibi if the Feds got her with that crew."

"Uh, huh." Slim was plainly absorbed. He unburdened himself a moment later. "Look, Captain—take what you got and quit this now. Tip the Feds off to the game and get out. I'm—scared."

Satan shrugged. "But, who is Simmiss? Sure—I turn his name in, and then what? He disappears...just as all his 'clients' do. Then there's a criminal not brought to justice—a man free to start the racket over again, probably in some more subtle way. No, Slim. I'm in this and I stay in until I get Simmiss; or he gets me. Simmiss will come to me when he hears I'm muscling in!"

Slim added despondently, "Or when the Feds get you, or the local cops get you." But he gave the argument up.

A PRIVATE ambulance stopped outside the apartment three hours later. Slim was summoned by Doc, went to speak to the doorman. "Sick patient from a hospital," he explained. "Special work to be done on her here."

"Sure," the functionary told the surprised Slim. "Doctor Simmiss has them now and then."

Satan went below stairs to the operating room, and Doc unveiled his purchase. Satan nodded his head. "Looks like the pictures I've seen of Carfano, all right." He turned. "Can you handle it okay, Dutchman?"

The big fellow was pale but he made his inspection, with Doc's help, then consulted his charts. "I can handle it," he said after a pause. "I'm glad Carfano likes gold teeth. That simplifies the job. Of course, you'll appreciate that this takes time?"

"How long?"

"If I work steadily… early to-morrow morning."

"Get going, Dutchman. There'll be a bonus for you and Doc, for this."

Satan and Slim retired to the office and made a minute study of charts of the Tombs jail. They called for Big Bill and got first hand information on the routine of the place—a detention prison for men awaiting Grand Jury action, or trial.

When they were alone again, Satan said: "It looks as if we'll have to do our work in the prison yard, Slim. You see—the jail takes up almost a full block, leaving this open yard for exercise. That's where the spring has to be staged."

Slim was puzzled. "But how about the corpse? You don't just drive a body into a jail and say 'Here y'are folks, we're trading even for Carfano.'"

Satan said, "Look, Slim: there never was a break from any jail that wasn't managed with bribery or because of the guards' laxity in the performance of their duties. You know that. A smuggled gun, or a saw that is slipped by—or any of a number of things. Now, the clever part of Simmiss' racket is that *after* that break, the prisoners are apparently all accounted for—*with the Simmiss client dead!* There's no search—because there's nothing to search for."

"But how did Simmiss get those bodies in?"

Satan shrugged. "I'd like to know, myself. But right now, my problem is to get this one into the Tombs. Let me worry with it, Slim. I'll call you later."

Slim went out and sank into a chair. He brooded over the

thing, but aroused himself at last to send Big Bill for the afternoon newspapers. He read that there were no new developments on the Burton Murnell murder. *An arrest is expected hourly,* the item said. Slim shook his head and turned the page.

Big Shot Prisoners Being Shifted, a headline proclaimed.

Slim straightened out the paper and sat up. The article continued:

> Because of the recent deaths in jail of Number One Public Enemies, the Attorney General, two days ago, ordered the transfer of many prominent Federal prisoners to Alcatraz Island in San Francisco Bay.
>
> One of these men, Pagan Lorando, big-time kidnaper doing time at Leavenworth Penitentiary, went into a mad rage and threatened the lives of the Attorney General and of Jo Desher, Chief of the Federal Bureau of Investigation, said to be responsible for the transfer order.

Slim whistled. He went rapidly to Satan's door and rapped. Inside, he shoved the paper into Satan's hand, pointed out the article.

Satan read, his eyes narrowing. He tossed the paper back onto his desk and thought for some time, his head in his hands. At last he looked up.

"This will settle it, Slim," he said with a sober face. "These snatch artists, Simmiss and his gang, will never crack Alcatraz. And all the rich ones are going there."

Slim's face brightened. "Then you'll call quits on this job?"

"I certainly won't. Simmiss is the biggest of the lot. And we'll find where Mikkle and Gilkane and Murrah are hiding out, when we get him. *Then* I'll quit—but only then! I'll call you when I've got things figured out."

The shadow of Satan appeared on the door!

LATE THAT night, Satan sat behind the desk in Simmiss' office and faced his tense crew, and Benny the Fog. Satan's face was taut, grim, his gray eyes flatly opaque. Deep lines of care and concentration cut his cheeks and forehead.

"You nearly through, Dutchman?"

The big man nodded, tight-lipped. Doc stirred at his side. "He's a marvelous workman, Cap'n. Marvelous! And don't kid yourself he hasn't innards."

Satan nodded. "We'll all need a lot of guts to carry off the plan I have laid out. Listen closely, all of you." He turned to Benny.

"Carfano got enough drag to see his lawyer at any reasonable time?"

The Fog nodded. "Dey tell me it looks like a convention, he has so many mout'-pieces swarmin' around dere."

"Good." Satan looked at his chart.

"You get word to one of the lawyers that Carfano must be out of that cell—between nine-thirty in the morning and ten o'clock. Understand?"

"I get it."

He held up another chart. "Here is the place, in the yard, where the prisoners are checked in. It's this small building. This flight of stairs—" he indicated a sketch on the chart—"leads to the cell block on the first floor, where Carfano is penned. There's a guard here, and a mesh door, at the top of the landing."

Benny the Fog was taking notes. "Shoot de works."

"That door will be open… with newly arrived prisoners coming through. And so will the one at the foot of the stairs."

"Yep."

"Carfano is to start back for his cell when he hears those men coming up. But instead of going to the cell, he will walk to the stairs and *down!*"

"But how about de screw? Will the screw let him?"

"Good, Benny! And that's the main part of this layout. Carfano is to pass word along the cell block that the rest of the prisoners are to raise hell when he gives the word. They're to raise and smash their bunks down on the chains; scream and shout and howl. That'll get the attention of his guard for a moment; long enough for Carfano to get to that door at the head of the stairs."

"When do dey start to holler? How do dey know when?"

"Tell Carfano, when he is near that door, to call out: 'No rough stuff now, boys!' And that's the tip-off for the riot to begin."

"An' he'll get down de steps O.K.?"

"If he's there, he'll get down O.K." Satan reached into his wallet and fetched out a hundred-dollar bill. "Say the whole thing over, Benny. Say it for the hundred."

The Fog repeated his instructions. Satan smiled and put the hundred back into his wallet. "You'll get that when you report back here tomorrow afternoon, Benny. I'm not taking any chances on your forgetting." He paused, stared keenly at the man.

"You hopped up now?"

The Fog shook his head. "Ain't been on de stuff in a year—since I come out o' de hospital."

Satan nodded. "Get going. And don't let anything slip, or—!"

The Fog was going out of the room when Satan's voice stopped him. "What news of Simmiss? Any?"

The go-between shrugged. "He's layin' low. But he knows by dis time dat you're in de racket. I told enough guys. But I got me lines out. I'll know where de guy is, soon enough."

When he had gone, Satan turned to Slim. "You got the uniforms?"

"Right, Captain. We'll only need one, though—for Big Bill."

"The patrol wagon?"

"Kayo tried out a uniform and stuck one up. It's in the warehouse now, gassed and set. Soapy's guarding it and the cop who was driving it."

Satan shook his head. "There's the weak point. They'll be looking for that Black Maria all over the city."

"Sure they will. But I had the numbers changed on this one. We grabbed the numbers of a broken-down bus, just to be sure we won't meet ourselves going down the street."

Satan stared at Slim for a long moment, then nodded. "It's only one of a number of chances we have to take. Now, attention, all of you, and let's get this thing straight. Then we'll have a dress rehearsal… right here. The first snatch of 'Sin, Incorporated,' is ready for the oven!"

CHAPTER 10
CARFANO GOES FOR A RIDE

THE NEXT morning, at exactly nine-thirty, a police wagon stopped outside the gate leading to the prison yard of the Tombs. The driver clanged the bell, and in a moment the guard at the gate, after looking through a slit in the steel, opened the big doors.

The driver of the big wagon said, "Hello, Patty. This is the load from the Fifty-Fourth Street Court. A fine bunch of lugs they are, too."

The van wheeled into the yard and drew up before a small house that was connected with the main building. A patrolman descended from the front seat and unlocked the rear doors. A line of men emerged and started, in single file, into the small building, preparatory to being assigned to cells.

The gates of the yard had barely closed, and the last few prisoners in the first wagon had just entered the building, when there was another persistent clang-clang from outside the gate. The guard, with an annoyed mutter, went again to the opening in the gate. He eyed the second patrol wagon standing there.

The driver, a big, pleasant-looking man, dressed in the uniform of a policeman, said to him, "This is the second load from Fifty-Fourth Street. They had a busy night up there."

The guard swung the gate open and the Black Maria pulled inside. Directly behind the police van was a long, low limousine, and it was driven in before the guard had a chance to close the gates.

"What the hell—" he started, but that was as far as he got. One of the doors opened swiftly and an automatic was pressed into his side. Soapy hissed.

"No chatter, now, Patty. Just keep your pants on and everything will be all right."

An expert hand ran over the guard and disarmed him, then he was yanked into the rear seat and thrust onto the floor. The car proceeded and drew up beside the second police wagon, which had stopped in front of the entrance and now pulled over to the side of the prison yard as soon as the limousine was in position.

From the big black car emerged four men, Satan, Slim, Doc and Gentleman Dan. Kayo remained at the wheel and Soapy held a gun on the prison guard in the back seat.

Each of the four held a tommy-gun, and as they went into the building, Satan flashed a shield to the guard at the door and noticed the other man at the desk.

"G-men," he said. "We heard there was a break planned for this morning—got the information through a stool pigeon. Thought you might like to have us around if anything happened."

The officer smiled. "We sure would, if anything happened. But we keep pretty close tab on them, in here. Nothing *ever* happens."

Satan permitted himself a wry smile. "You can never tell," he said.

He eyed the room quickly. At the other end was a door to a stairway that led to the upper floor. This, he knew, was the stair that Carfano would use in a few moments. The doors, steel-meshed, at both the top and bottom of the stairway, were still open. The last of the incoming prisoners was ascending them, followed by a guard.

He strode to the door leading into the yard and looked out. Everything was going perfectly. The police wagon they had stolen was about twenty yards away, towards the gate, and Big Bill was even now engaged in using a spray gun on the body of the van—a spray gun which, Satan knew, contained gasoline.

He went back into the room and saw that his crew had found it necessary to abandon their disguises. The two policemen had probably become suspicious. Now they had been disarmed and tied together in the corner.

"They smelled trouble," Slim said. "We had to make a package of them."

"Okay! Go out and get the other guard from the car and tie him with the others."

Doc moved to carry out the order.

"Where is Carfano? He ought to be making the break about now. They won't leave those doors open forever," Satan whipped impatiently.

As he spoke, a wild clamor broke out above them. There was the crashing of tin plates on bars; the slamming of prison bunks; the wild shouting of frenzied men.

And then they saw the figure running down the stairs. Satan recognized him instantly as Carfano. "This way!" he shouted, and the man came toward them.

Satan was near the door of the stairway, and as Carfano ran down into the room, he slammed the door shut. But not before he got a glimpse of what was going on in the cell block above him. The scene was one of riot. The din was terrific, and in the excitement, one other prisoner bedsides Carfano had gotten loose. He was making a break for the stairs, but one of the guards raised his tommy-gun and it stuttered sharply. The man clutched the bars of a cell and sank slowly to the floor.

As the door closed, the group whirled into activity. Satan rasped:

"Doc, into the car with Carfano! Dan, go down and get that outside gate open! Slim, you and I will see that there's no interference from this quarter."

They flashed into action, and Satan and Slim backed slowly out the door. At the entrance, Satan pulled a tear gas bomb from his pocket and threw it into the room.

Then they were in the yard. Kayo had turned the car around, and Big Bill had already thrown a match to the police wagon, which was standing near the outside wall. Satan noticed, with satisfaction, the rope ladder that had been thrown over the high concrete barricade. Even as he watched, Big Bill hauled the prepared corpse from the inside of the flaming police van and hurled it to the roof of the blazing vehicle. It would be a simple story to the prison authorities. Carfano, they would think, had tried to scale the wall, had slipped, and fallen onto the burning patrol wagon.

But the gate was open, now, and the car was rolling towards it swiftly. Slim had gathered the tommy-guns and thrown them into the flames. Satan paused long enough to hurl three smoke bombs into the yard to hide their immediate movements, then ran for the street. The car slowed up and waited for him.

He had reached the curb and was about to enter the crowded limousine when the policeman on the corner post, attracted by the noise and the shooting, ran up to them, drawing his gun as he came.

"What's going on here?" he demanded, and Satan spoke to him swiftly:

"We're G-men, officer. We're just taking—"

HE STOPPED abruptly as, out of the corner of his eye, he noticed a long, blue touring car creeping silently down the street towards them. In the front seat sat a man he knew well—a man who was clean-shaven, now, but with those unmistakable, strange green eyes. Satan instantly noted the ugly snouts of the two machine guns that protruded over the edge of the car.

"Get going, Kayo!" he snarled. "It's Simmiss and his gang!" The big limousine immediately shot away from the curb.

Satan dove for his automatic as the machine guns started to clatter. The patrolman lunged at him, bringing his gun up. But Satan slammed it aside and fired under the man's arm.

"Not me, you fool," he shouted. "The worst killer in the country is in that car behind you!"

The copper swung, only half convinced. A slug hit him high on the shoulder. Gamely, he switched the service automatic to his left hand and opened fire. Satan, at his side, backed the man against the wall.

Simmiss' gunmen were having trouble. The gun of one of them had jammed and he was cursing frantically and batting at the thing with one hand. The other tried twice to get his weapon trained on Satan and the cop again. Both times he was thrown off his aim by the panicky movements of his companion.

Satan fired twice, slowly. The man with the good gun fell forward, his chin catching on the side of the door. He lolled there, his mouth open, while blood streamed from a hole between his eyes.

"Good going," the cop growled as he tried to get a bead on the other. "You sure saved my life, buddy!" He was firing for the front seat. The windshield shattered in a thousand pieces and Simmiss dived under the dashboard of the car.

Satan moved with the slowly rolling automobile, fired again and again. The gunner with the jammed weapon screamed suddenly. He dropped the tommy-gun and clutched at his chest. Slowly, he slid forward to the floor of the car.

The big car jumped ahead at terrific speed, nearly knocking two pedestrians down. People were fleeing for cover all over the streets, diving into the Court building, throwing themselves prone on the sidewalks, flattening up against the walls, and ducking behind parked automobiles.

The killers' car tore at increasing speed across Lafayette Street as a police siren screamed from somewhere. Satan heard the gates at his back start to swing open. He grabbed the policeman and yanked him along as he ran down the street.

"We'll get a car and go after them!" he barked.

At the corner, a frightened taxi driver was slumped down in

his seat, his face white. Satan jerked open the door of the cab. "Go after that blue car," he ordered, showing his badge.

The copper looked faint. Satan saw the other policemen ranging up on him. He pushed the policeman back. "I'll go after them. You stay here and get your shoulder fixed." He stepped into the cab and stuck his gun into the back of the driver's neck.

"Get going!"

The taxi driver slammed into second gear, then ripped across the street, just in front of a truck. The truck driver cursed and stood up on his brakes. His motor stalled.

Satan's taxi careened down the street, the police cars in back sirening and their occupants howling to the truckman to clear a passage for them. At the corner, Satan's driver turned left. One block up, Satan barked, "Left! Turn left! Take me uptown to Headquarters!"

As the car slued back into Lafayette Street, Satan dropped the gun into his pocket and brought out his wallet. He jammed a twenty-dollar bill into the driver's license frame, leaving one end out so the man would see it when later he examined the rear.

At Canal Street, Satan snapped: "I think I see one of those fellows now. Hold it here. Right by this subway entrance. Wait for me!" He jumped down, leaving the door open, and rounded the corner of the subway entrance.

He went down the steps with his feet twinkling, jammed a nickel into the turnstile slot and sped to the train level. Two minutes later, a train ground to a stop and Satan got aboard. The train pulled out.

At Fourteenth Street he got out, crossed over the station bridge, and climbed into a downtown express. He emerged several stations further on and went to the street. For several hours he sat in a restaurant, stirring and stirring the coffee which he ordered but never drank.

The noonday luncheon crowds were in the streets when Satan went out and boarded a taxi.

"The overhead highway to Twenty-Third Street," he said. "Then, up Eleventh Avenue to Forty-Ninth, and east until I tell you to stop."

SATAN MADE his way into the Simmiss offices where he faced his grim crew.

He nodded tensely. "Nice going, boys!" He looked to the chair where Nick Carfano sat, his thick-lipped, sullen face turned up to Satan. But he ignored him. "Four minutes, I estimate, from the time we went in until the gates closed on us again."

No one spoke. Satan took off his coat and threw it onto a table. Carfano stretched, yawned and arose.

"Gimme a drink and a cigarette, and when do I get out of here?"

"You can have a drink and a smoke," Satan told him. "But— you *don't* get out of here."

"Huh?" The stocky blackmailer stared. "Whaddya mean, I don't get out of here? Is this a gag? Ain't I paid already?"

Satan smiled coldly. "You paid to get out of the Tombs," he said. "I got you out. But what I do with you now is my business."

"You double-crossin', yellow livered—"

"Shut up, you," Satan snarled. "Shut up or I'll give you what's coming to you! You rat!" He paused, his eyes ugly and boring into the man. "All your rotten life you've made things hell for other people; blackmailing, torturing, killing, even, I suppose. I made a contract with your go-between—to spring you from the Tombs. I sprang you. But if I hear any more out of you, you'll wish I'd left you there!"

Carfano's skin was a dirty white when he dropped his eyes from Satan's.

The leader turned to Slim. "Truss this bird, gag and blindfold him. Then set him down—you know where. That patrol wagon driver might have a few nice things to say to him.

Carfano licked his thick lips. "Look, you—I don't even know who you are. But there's a hundred 'gees' in it for you if you think this over and see it my way."

"Not for a million," Satan told him.

After Carfano had been tied and gagged and placed in another room until dark would fall, and it was safe to take him out, Satan called Slim aside.

"Simmiss came to me," he said. "As I thought he would. But sooner than I was ready for him. We'll wait until the newspapers are out on the street and see how the thing went."

Slim nodded. "What puzzles me is, won't the police figure out that the corpse we left isn't Carfano?"

Satan shrugged. "We'll have to wait and see." He paused; then: "It's my guess, Slim, that it will get by. And drive Simmiss into the open!"

103

CHAPTER 11
CRIME, COAST TO COAST

I T WAS late in the afternoon when Gentleman Dan went down to the corner and came back with the newspapers. He turned them over to Slim and the lieutenant of the crew took them into Simmiss' office. Satan was sitting there alone, his gray eyes veiled by the smoke that arose from the cigarette in his hand.

Satan opened one. Across the top of the front page, in scare-head type, was:

TOMBS JAIL BREAK FOILED.

Satan looked at Slim and dropped his eyes to the paper again. *Nick Carfano Dead After Spectacular Escape Fails,* another headline read.

"I'll read it," Satan said.

The article ran:

Early this morning, the Tombs prison at Franklin and Centre Streets was the scene of a daring attempt to free Nick Carfano, master-mind blackmailer, awaiting Grand Jury action. Carfano, who was refused bail, had been interviewing one of his attorneys and was on the way back to his cell when a disturbance occurred in the cell block. Carfano made a dive for the door through which some new prisoners were passing.

Some mobsters, suspected to be Carfano's own gang, gained entry to the jail yard through the clever trick of appearing in a patrol van. The gateman was completely taken in. Some of the gunmen posed as G-men, another was uniformed as a policeman.

With the aid of some tear gas bombs and smoke bombs, the gunmen got Carfano into the jail yard and on his way to freedom. A rope ladder had been thrown up on one of the walls and smoke bombs hurled around to make a screen under which Carfano could make his escape. The fugitive had climbed up on the stolen van, which had been left by the wall, and was apparently overcome by smoke there.

In some way the van caught fire—perhaps from a bomb—and the blackmailer was burned to death—only feet away from an escape.

An ironic twist is that Carfano's henchmen made their escape through the same gate they used in entering the place. A wild gun battle on the streets followed, when a blue touring car carrying machine gunners took revenge on the police for the failure to free Carfano.

Police are seeking the identity of a mysterious G-man who saved a policeman's life and fought the gunmen off single-handed.

Carfano's body was so badly burned that positive identification cannot be made until Carfano's personal dentist—Dr. Michael Giffontis—calls at Headquarters with his records, showing the exact dental work that he had done on the criminal's mouth.

The rest of the papers were of the same tenor.
Satan shook his head. "There you are," he said. "But—there's

one thing I'd stake my life on. Nothing short of magic or bribery got corpses into those Federal pens."

Slim nodded. "That's the way it seems. But—" He stopped when a whistling sound announced that someone was calling from downstairs on the speaking tube. He answered it.

"Benny the Fog is on his way up the back steps."

"Bring him in," Satan ordered.

The go-between came in stealthily and slid into a chair. "Dat wuz some spring," he said, admiringly. *"Some* spring! Plenty o' dressin', plenty o' noise! De publicity will help get more jobs!"

Satan nodded, pulled out his wallet and tossed Benny the Fog one hundred dollars.

"An' another 'gee,'" Benny said softly.

"What do you mean?" Satan asked, his eyes hard. "For what?"

"You gimme half a 'gee' de night before last, huh? An' you said it was doubles if I found where dis guy Simmiss was hidin'?"

Satan sat forward in his chair. "You know?"

"Uh, huh." The Fog stared meaningly at the wallet. Satan counted out a thousand dollars and shoved it to Benny the Fog. "Spill it," he snapped.

The Fog looked carefully around him, then slid a piece of folded paper across the desk. "I don't even want to say it!" he whispered. "But—it's de McCoy!"

"You wait here," Satan told the man. He went out and called Slim. "I know where Simmiss is! We'll take a chance and bundle Carfano down to the warehouse now. Send Gentleman Dan with him. Tell him to stay there, on guard, with Soapy; until he hears from us again.

"Get the boys set, Slim! We're going after our friend Simmiss!"

An hour later, Benny the Fog walked through the empty apartment, helped himself to some food, downed three drinks, smoked a cigar; and stretched out on a bed for a sleep until Satan and his crew would return.

SATAN NUDGED Kayo to stop while they were still a block from the address that Benny the Fog had given them.

The second car drove ahead slowly and stopped a block beyond. Both groups climbed down and converged on the house they were seeking. Near the door, Satan stopped his men. "I'll go on alone," he said. "I want to pass the house once and take a look… see what the set-up is like."

The others made themselves scarce while Satan walked ahead and looked the place over. It was an old-fashioned type of house, with a high, brownstone stoop. All the shades were closely drawn. Satan walked on and came up to the second group.

"Pat," he ordered. "You skirt around to the back and see if you can get in there." He turned. "Big Bill—stumble up those steps. Act as though you were drunk. Shout that you want a dime, or a cup of coffee. That'll stir up something. We'll see if those eggs are answering the door."

Tensely, the crew waited. Big Bill put on a good drunken act and staggered up the steps. He pulled the old bell and banged on the closed storm doors. But there was no sign of life in the place. Satan was shifting impatiently when the sound of a dull explosion came from the house… and another. Then, silence.

But a minute later, the storm doors were swung open and Pat stuck his head out. The crew swarmed up the steps and inside, pulling the doors shut after them. In the hall on the first floor, lying up against the wall where he fell, was the man who had been with Costa and Simmiss in the cellar of the downtown place.

There was an ugly hole in his right cheek, and blood was pouring from a wound in his neck. Satan went over and knelt near him, stared at the man. Slowly, the wounded mobster's eyes came open. Satan picked up the gun the man had dropped and leaned close.

"Who else is in this house? Where are they?"

The man stared at Satan, recognition dawning in his dimming eyes. "You—devil!" he gasped weakly. "You—human devil. I'd hoped they had you by now!"

"Hoped who had me?" Satan asked.

"The—mob," the man whispered. "They—left me—and went after—*you!*"

"Where?"

The wounded man shook his head. "You'll—know soon enough."

Satan looked up at Slim. "The warehouse?" He shook the man. "I don't want to hurt you any worse than you're hurt now," he snapped. "But I intend to hear where your mob went!"

Slim said, "I'll send Kayo down to the—" But he stopped, his head cocked to one side. Satan rose to his feet, his eyes on the stairs that led up to the second story.

Muffled sounds, as of someone kicking and struggling, came to them where they stood. Satan barked, "Get out your guns and climb those stairs. Go easy, now! It may be an ambush!"

He stood tense, his eyes raised to that other floor. The sounds had ceased again. Satan's men tramped from room to room, then mounted to the third story of the house. Pat came alongside the leader.

"I jimmied a window and found the guy cocking his gun and getting ready to yank Bill in and let him have it. So I gave him the works."

Satan nodded, then said in a low voice: "He's dying. I wonder—?"

A shout came from upstairs, then a yell down to Satan. "It's a woman, Cap'n! Tied up and stuck into a closet. The rest of the house is empty!"

"Bring her down," Satan ordered. He listened to the crew descend, saw them round the bend in the stairs. In the lead were Slim and Kayo, supporting between them a woman who was too weak to walk. They came on slowly.

It was Wanda Mellin, Simmiss' assistant!

THEN MINUTES later, Wanda Mellin had responded to restoratives given her by Doc. She was sitting in a chair with her head back and her eyes closed. Once she opened them and smiled wanly at Satan. Doc looked from the girl to his chief, then back again, adoration plain in his eyes.

Satan drew a chair near her and sank into it. "Feeling better?"

"Yes," the girl whispered, her eyes coming open again. "Oh, that—that beast of a man! I felt sure you'd come… somehow… after I heard you'd escaped."

"Where are they now?"

"On the way to the office," she whispered. "They watched

109

the place, to see if the police were after them. And—they knew you were there."

Satan swung to Slim. "My God! I told Benny the Fog to wait there for me!" He turned to Wanda. "How long ago did they leave?"

The girl hesitated, pondering. "Perhaps an hour ago," she said.

Satan puzzled the thing. "Benny would have heard them coming and could have got out the front," he said. "I told him to wait in the front room there." He turned back to Wanda. "When will they be back? Did they mention that fact?"

The girl shook her head. "They're—not coming back. Not until after they had freed—" She paused, frowning. "Someone they said would be their last job. I don't remember the name."

Satan frowned. "All we can do is wait," he said, his eyes going to Slim. "Wait for them *here!* I guess it means they won't be back today, at any rate." He thought a minute. "Slim—you take the boys, with the exception of Doc, and get down there to the office. Maybe you'll be in time, but I doubt it. Leave one car here. If you can see them from the street, 'phone me here. I saw a 'phone in the hall when I came in. I guess it's working. Try it."

Slim went out. He came in again and said, "The 'phone is O.K. I've taken the number. Suppose they are there?"

Satan's face was grim. "Stand guard, and wait for Doc and me. We'll make a finish of this thing, once and for all!"

When they had gone, Satan looked at the girl curiously.

"How did you ever come to get mixed up with this crowd? And when did they start tying you up?"

"I've—always wanted to work in a doctor's office," the girl said. "I was passing Dr. Simmiss' offices a little over a month ago, and thought I'd apply for a job, whenever he had a vacancy. It looked like a respectable place."

Satan's face was hard. "It looked it, all right. Then what?"

"He hired me right away. It wasn't until a week later that I went downstairs and saw a—a *body* on that table—saw them doing something to its teeth. I knew it was dead, from the horrible way its eyes looked at me, and the way its legs and arms were twisted."

Satan nodded. "We know the whole story, now. Then what?"

"After that, Dr. Simmiss made me stay there, gave me a room. He—he didn't bother me—in any way—until we came up here. I—" the girl shuddered and hid her face in her hands. "I clawed him to ribbons, his face, when he came near me. He struck me and had me tied up and thrown in that closet." She looked up, tearful. "Don't let him find me here when he comes back! I'm—"

Doc interrupted, his voice savage. "I'll tear him apart with my bare hands," he said. "He made a pass at you, did he? Why, the dirty—" The medico paused, his face red, and looked at Satan.

"Don't mind me," Satan said mildly. "I'm used to my crew beating my time. Gentleman Dan did it last. They're great guys with the girls."

Wanda blushed and said, "I think you're both very nice."

"Thanks," Satan grinned. "But I don't have a doctor's office

111

that you can work in, whereas our friend here—" He bowed to Doc and went out of the room.

THE MAN in the hall was dead, and Satan came back in the room after making a thorough inspection of the house. "There's nothing to be found," he said to Doc. "I've searched all over, and can't find a thing. If they're working on another 'spring,' they're fixing the evidence some other place or—"

Wanda cut in. "They said they were going to—er—*muscle* it? Is that the word? I heard them talking it over."

"Oho," Satan said. "Desperate, are they? Probably one last job and they're going to lie low for a while."

Wanda nodded. "I don't know who the man is they are after. They mentioned his name. But they are to meet a man named Dippy Jake, or Jake the Dip, or something, near a place called Tiburton."

"*What?*" Satan was on his feet again, leaning over the girl. He shook her by the shoulder roughly. "Not—*Tiburon?*"

Wanda nodded her head. "Yes. That's it. They said they'd 'blast the cars to heaven.' Only, they didn't say heaven! Does that help?"

"Does it help?" Satan swung to Doc. "Tiburon is the old railroad station that was taken over by the government as the shipping off spot for the Alcatraz-bound cars. They roll the railroad cars onto barges there."

Wanda spoke again. "I heard so many names," she said. "I've been trying to remember the man they're to 'spring' how. Could it have been—" she hesitated a moment, " 'Heathen' somebody-or-other?"

112

Satan blinked. "Heathen? Heathen?" Then a look of incredulity passed over his face. "Pagan!" he shouted. *"Pagan Lorando!"*

"Yes, that's it!"

"My God!" Satan breathed. "Simmiss is on his way to the Alcatraz shipping point to blast the cars that Pagan Lorando is riding in. You know? The man who threatened to get loose and kill the Attorney-General and Jo Desher, head of the F.B.I.?"

Doc nodded. "But they haven't got time."

Wanda said, "They mentioned something about flying."

"They're flying out there!" Satan barked. "Flying to spring Pagan Lorando right from the jaws of Alcatraz! Why, it's the most amazing thing I've ever heard!"

"He'll do it," Wanda said. "Try, anyway. Dr. Simmiss is insane, Mr. Satan."

Doc guffawed at the strange title. But Satan stood immobile, his face frozen. He was standing that way five minutes later when the telephone rang. Satan answered the 'phone and recognized the voice that said, "Captain?"

"Right, Slim."

"I'm not at the office. We drove up near there, and found a couple of hundred cops."

"Go on, Slim. What's the rest of it?"

"I dug up a rookie copper and slipped him a piece of cash; told him I was a feature writer and wanted the story. I got it."

"Well?"

Slim's voice came very low over the wire. "The apartment of a Dr. Simmiss was machine-gunned, and when the cops got there, they found a man dead on one of the beds—his tongue cut out and an ivory-handled knife stuck in his heart. He was was an underworld character called Benny the Fog!"

LATE THAT night, one of the pilots at Newark Air Terminal watched a big transport plane trundle down a runway to its take-off position.

"What's that crate hopping off for?" he asked a dispatcher.

"Chartered job. Some shoe manufacturers, late for that convention in 'Frisco," was the answer.

"Pretty good," the pilot said. "Business is O.K. The regular Transcontinental had to put on an extra section for those other eggs who came out a couple of hours ago. This'll beat 'em in, though."

"Yeah," the dispatcher said. He was staring at the chartered plane as it thundered along on its take-off. "That guy with the tough gray eyes who arranged this deal must have dough to burn. He offered the pilot, Nibs Mackley, a thousand bucks for every hour he cut from his best previous time. Must be in a hurry to get there."

"And for why?" the pilot laughed. "Who'll ever know the difference?"

NEARING CLEVELAND, Satan signaled Slim to come to the rear of the ship.

"Here's the dope on Alcatraz," he said in a low voice. "See if you think anyone's ever going to get out of *that!*"

Slim read the details of "The Rock"... A mile and a half north of the San Francisco docks, and just inside the Golden Gate.... Twelve acres of chisel-proof metal and rock and cement, one hundred and eighty feet up out of the waters of San Francisco Bay.... Seven hundred yards, more or less, from stem to stern....

Barbed-wire entanglements, 'honor' guards watching the criminals, no more than two convicts permitted to stand in a group during the exercise periods, foolproof entries to the cells with door after door to be opened and closed before you get on to the cell block. Mirrors in the ceilings overhead, loud speaker equipment for communication between criminals and their visitors; no whispered conferences here: plate glass between the visitor and the convict. No passing of weapons or tools for escape here! Metal-detectors at the gates to the prison, so that the presence of even a pin head will register, if a visitor is trying to smuggle something in.

"It's neat," Slim said. "Pagan and his little playmates will be safe enough there. That fixes Simmiss for keeps, I guess."

Satan looked down from the window at the lights of Cleveland, wheeling beneath their wings. "Yes, Slim. But unless we stop Simmiss, he'll fix those guards and convicts for keeps—with his crazy idea that he can blast Pagan Lorando loose and make one final killing!"

CHAPTER 12
BIG BILL SAY GOOD-BY

S ATAN AND his crew unloaded at the San Francisco terminal of the air line and climbed stiff-legged down the landing platform. Satan pulled Slim to one side. "With Doc and Gentleman Dan and Soapy left behind, there's only seven of us. I want the crew to hang together as much as possible. At all times."

"Yes, Captain."

"But we've got to tail Simmiss and his gang when they come in. Through them, we can get a line on this Jake the Dip that Wanda spoke about. He's evidently the money man out here for the Pagan Lorando mob. Meantime, set a man on the Dip's trail and find just who he is."

Slim blinked. "You're not figuring on trying to get Lorando yourself, are you?"

"Do you think I'm crazy?" Satan asked. "If these crooks have any money lying around loose, I'm going to make a try at getting it. That's all. I'll take the dough, but what do I do with Lorando?"

"Right, Captain. I'll put Sol on the Simmiss gang, and send Big Bill out to see what he can nose up about Jake the Dip. I'll tell 'em what hotel they can find us at. I'll send them now."

When Slim had detailed the men, The Dutchman, Pat, Kayo and Satan joined him and piled their weary frames into an automobile. It was beyond dinnertime when they arrived at the small hotel which Satan had chosen for their stay.

"Slim and I will stay here," Satan told the other three. "You men go out and eat. Bring some coffee and sandwiches back for us."

"Right, Cap'n."

When they were alone, Satan stared at Slim for a long time. Finally he stirred, lighted a cigarette and blew a cloud of smoke ceilingward. "We've been together a long time, Slim," he said. "But I don't know when we've had less to go on than we have now. All we know is, Simmiss is going to make a mad try at springing Pagan Lorando."

Slim sat forward. "Captain? Why not just tip the Feds and chuck this thing now?"

Satan shook his head. "No go. I have a hunch that Simmiss has a trick up his sleeve that we don't know about. He's my game now. I'll tail him like a bloodhound until I find out what it is!"

The other three came back in a short time and Slim and Satan drank some coffee. Slim was about to lie down for a little sleep when the 'phone rang. He answered it, then signaled to Satan.

"It's Big Bill," he said. "He wants you."

Satan went to the instrument and listened intently. Then he said, "You stick there until you see if Simmiss shows up. He's more important to watch than Jake the Dip. He's green-eyed and his arm is in a sling. You can't miss him. But be careful!"

When he turned, he said, "Big Bill asked for Jake the Dip and got the evil eye. He called a friend, and was told to go to a saloon called Greasy Joe's. Bill says he's sure the man is there, or will be there. Simmiss doesn't know him, so he's safe."

Several hours later, Sol called. "Both planes are in. Simmiss is on the second one. And what a tough looking guy! But, Cap'n—know who was on the first section?"

Satan tensed. "Who?"

"That big G-man—Jo Desher. Yeah! He hustled right off as soon as the plane got in!"

Satan thought a moment. Then: "You follow Simmiss, and

if he goes to a hotel, wait right outside. Big Bill is in place at Greasy Joe's, waiting to see if Simmiss contacts Jake the Dip. He's Pagan Lorando's go-between in this deal. Got that straight?"

"Right, Cap'n."

Satan turned to Slim when he had hung up the 'phone. "Desher just blew into town—on the same schedule with Simmiss, but on the first of the two planes."

"My God!" Slim breathed. "Then—he left before we did? Our plane made better time than the regular transports."

A bullet from the big
car winged the copper.

Satan nodded. "He must be jittery about Pagan, after all those other things that have happened to big racketeers. My bet," he paused and licked his lips, "my bet is that he is going to board that convict train and ride to Alcatraz with the prisoners. To make sure they get there!"

It was two hours later that the telephone rang again. Satan jumped up from he bed where he was lying fully clothed and answered it.

"Who? Sol? Go ahead, Sol. What is it?" His voice was low and tense.

He listened for some time, then said, "No. Don't tag them any longer. Come right over here to the hotel." He dropped the receiver back on the hook.

"Sol says that Simmiss and four men who came with him are at Greasy Joe's. He lost him when he left the hotel, picked him up there later. A man Sol believes to be Jake the Dip passed an envelope to Simmiss. The five of them came out then. Sol hid, heard Simmiss tell the driver to go to Laub's Boatyard."

Satan paused, his eyes heavy. He poured a glass of water and downed it. Slim was watching him closely.

"What about Big Bill, Captain?"

"Big Bill wasn't at Greasy Joe's when Sol got there. Sol thought maybe he was hiding around in back of the place. He circled the joint and found Big Bill in the alleyway behind it.

"Big Bill is dead with an ivory-handled knife sticking out of his back."

IT WAS after two in the morning when Satan and his crew

left the shady funeral parlor in a poorer section of the city and started for the boatyard.

Big Bill's remains were being prepared for shipment to New York, the undertaker having been well paid for his efforts in getting a "heart failure" certificate from a physician he knew.

In the car, Slim sat in moody silence. Once he stirred and said: "Big Bill was a right guy. We'll go a long time before we find another like him."

"See that his family gets the break on this," Satan ordered. "Half my share goes to them, Slim." After a moment, he turned to Sol:

"You say Simmiss and his gang loaded some boxes into their car at Greasy Joe's?"

Sol nodded. He was visibly shaken. Satan fell into a moody silence that wasn't broken until they were near the boatyard. There he called a halt.

"We'll go on foot from here," he said. "Be careful, all of you. Simmiss will have a guard on that dock, if he's up to anything. Keep your eyes peeled and your guns handy!"

Satan circled far to the right of the road. He made his way cautiously through a sparsely wooded sector, then along behind some decrepit shacks. The smell of the salty water grew stronger in his nostrils. Farther on, the land sloped abruptly and he came to a clearing. He stopped, his eyes glued to a cluster of lights ahead and to the left.

A husky signal bellowed, off to the right. Satan knew it was the warning-horn for ships on Alcatraz Island. He squatted down on his haunches and pulled a pair of night binoculars

121

from his pocket. Then he trained them on the lighted dock below.

At first he could make out nothing unusual. But soon he discerned a shadowy-figure lurking in the shadows of the boat-house. The figure turned now and again to stare up the road from the dock. Then it would retreat into the shadows and be still.

Suddenly a beam of light stabbed into the dark as the shack door was thrown open and a number of men came out. Satan trained his night glasses on the group. He saw them stop, bend low near the side of the wharf. One man jumped down. A moment later came the roar of a high-powered motor. Then another, loud in the still of the night. The twin motors purred.

"By God," Satan muttered. "A speedboat. Is he really—?"

Two more figures dropped down from the wharf. The speed-boat moved out from the wharf, with a giant ray of light guiding its way. The swirling water cascaded left and right.

The boat made perhaps two miles, then returned swiftly to the dock. Satan watched the men on the dock moor the craft. The group went back into the shack again.

"Making their plans, testing every angle," Satan guessed. "But does the fool think he's going to charge Alcatraz with that speed boat and take it by storm? With only four men to help him? Simmiss is crazy!"

For a moment, Satan considered making a surprise attack on the wharf. But he held back. The death of Big Bill made him hesitate to risk any more of his men. And, in addition, Satan was tempted to give Simmiss all the rope he wanted. *If* this was Simmiss down there.

And as he debated the thing, the door swung open again and another figure showed itself—a figure that stood huge in the light of the shack door; and a figure whose right arm was lying loosely in a sling.

It was Simmiss!

Simmiss signaled his men and pointed up the road in the dark. Satan's hair rose on his neck. He was afraid that one of his men had been discovered, lurking near that wharf.

But he sank back a moment later when the men walked to the back of the pier. One of them swung a flashlight that revealed an automobile parked in the dark. In a few minutes, the men started forward again, walking carefully, carrying between them a flat, square box.

Handling it gingerly, they lowered it off the side of the dock into the boat. They returned to the car and repeated the performance.

"Ammunition," Satan guessed. "They probably told Laub they were getting bait or booze for a fishing trip."

Satan had seen enough. He made his way back to his own car. He touched the light switch, snapped it once, then again. He waited.

Slim ranged up first; the others followed. They piled back into the car. Kayo eased it away as silently as a horse and buggy, until they were several miles from the wharf. Then he slipped it into high and made for the city. "To the hotel," Satan told

Kayo. Then he said to Sol: "What took you so long? You were the last one getting back. I warned you to watch for that signal!"

"Right, Cap'n," Sol said. "But you told us to get as close up as we could, didn't you? I was so near that car when they unloaded the stuff that I could have spit on those guys."

"Too risky," Satan told the little man. "You might have been caught."

"I wanted to hear them, if I could, Cap'n."

"But you didn't."

"But I did, Cap'n! They're using two boats, because I heard one of the men say 'The soup goes in the big boat.'"

Satan swung, his eyes blazing. "Soup?" He stared at Slim. "Do you think—?"

"Dynamite? Why not? They said they'd blast the cars, didn't they?"

Satan fell silent. But near the hotel he slammed his hand down on his knee. "Two boats! And dynamite! Slim—I think I have his scheme figured at last!"

Upstairs, he said to Sol and The Dutchman, "You fellows are going to stick here and send Big Bill's coffin through to New York. You go back on the train." He turned. "You—Kayo and Pat—get some sleep. Then get out to the airport in the morning and book passage for *four* of us on the Transcontinental. If Slim and I aren't there when the plane pulls out, you two hop it anyway."

"Aw, Cap'n!" Kayo wailed. "Aren't we going to be in on the killing?"

"Sometimes," Satan told the two veterans, "the killing is on the wrong side!"

PAT AND Kayo scowled and fell into despondent silence. Satan stared down on the deserted streets, turned suddenly and picked up the telephone book. He thumbed through the pages, called a number.

He waited for several minutes, smoking a cigarette and tapping his foot impatiently on the floor. Suddenly he sat erect.

"Hello? This you, Hank?... Now, wait a minute!... I know it's late, too.... Who am I?... Hank—I can't mention names, and I don't want you to mention any.... I'm the chap who pulled you out of a bad mess in Singapore a number of years ago.... Remember?"

Satan nodded his head vigorously and smiled tightly while he listened to the man on the other end. Then he spoke again.

"No, Hank.... I can't see you, not this trip.... But I want you to do me a favor, Hank.... It's a matter of life or death to a number of people.... Do you understand?... You've always had a lot to do with boats, Hank?... Well, I want the fastest boat I can get, and I want to drive it myself.... I'll pay for any damage I may do, naturally; and I'll tell you frankly that it may be *plenty* damaged....

"Who has it and where—?... *What!* You have it?... Well, that sort of makes things easier, doesn't it?... I'll be at your house in ten minutes!"

Satan dropped the receiver back and turned to Slim. "Pack. Let Kayo and Pat take our bags. All we'll want will be our guns and a fond prayer! I'm going to see if I can't stop this madman's try. It's worth an effort, anyway!"

When they were packing, he said to Kayo: "You'll drive us to where we're going and drop us. I can get the use of a car there. Turn this automobile back to the rental people and taxi to the airport."

"Right, Cap'n."

"Happy hunting," Satan said to the veteran when they stepped down from the car.

"Happy hunting, Cap'n," Kayo answered huskily.

"Happy fishing would be more like it, where we're going," Slim said drily.

CHAPTER 13
THE LAST BREAK

THE FIRST streaks of dawn were in the sky when a long, mahogany craft shot away from a private dock and nosed along the shore of San Francisco Bay.

Satan, at the wheel of the speedster, eased himself more comfortably down behind the windshield. He was helmeted and goggled, and clothed warmly in a cover-all with a cork life-preserver trussed around him. Slim, tall and gaunt at his side, was in identical attire.

The crisp winter air tore at their cheeks as Satan gunned the motors up slightly, and the speed craft sat its stern flatter into the water. The Golden Gate showed in the background. Behind that climbed the majestic mountains. Satan swirled the boat to the left, then passed his binoculars to Slim.

"You know the location of that boatyard. See if you can get it. Keep your eyes glued on it and tell me when you see anything come out."

He veered the craft right and left, gently, getting used to the feel of the thing. Then he headed for Alcatraz, "The Rock"—lying like a battleship near the mouth of the Gate. Satan glued his eyes on the place.

Slim sat suddenly straighter, wiped the lenses of the glasses and trained them on shore again. "I got the wharf!" he exclaimed.

Satan veered off line again, swung towards Tiburon. Far down the line he made out a bulky shape lying close to the water. He squinted his eyes. "Slim! What's that down there?"

Slim swung his glasses and looked. "A barge," he said slowly. "A barge with two… three… four railroad cars on it. And some sort of… a tug is towing it. And there's a larger boat alongside!"

"A Coast Guard cutter," Satan said. He took the binoculars and looked. "That's the boatload! They run the cars onto barges at Tiburon and haul them down. That saves going through 'Frisco; less chance of a 'snatch.'"

Slim shook his head. "Not to Simmiss' way of thinking." He swung the binocs shoreward again, shouted: "Here comes a boat out of that wharf! *Two* boats! One's a big devil—long. The other is a short job."

"Here they come," Satan said grimly, as he twisted the wheel. "I bet ten to one that Simmiss is in the smaller boat! With a helper!"

Slim shook his head. "Can't see," he muttered. But he kept the glasses trained as the two boats swung into the clear and sped along.

Satan steered off to the port side, as if to tell those two boats, should anyone in them be watching, "We're just kidding around!" But he wasn't fooling around. He was watching the movements of those boats as a vulture watches his prey.

Suddenly, the longer and faster of those two boats, sped up. It seemed fairly to leap clear of the water. Satan notched his throttle up and cut slightly in to the right. He, too, was racing down on the barge and the coast guard cutter. The pace was terrific.

Satan's craft squatted its stern end flatter and flatter as he slammed the throttle full open. He glanced at the speedometer, saw that they were booming through the water at better than fifty-five knots—about a mile a minute. A puff of white smoke plumed up from the cutter's funnel.

"The warning whistle," Satan shouted above the roar of the motors. "The cutter is warning that other speedboat to keep clear!"

But Simmiss' powerful craft plunged on, bow high, with the small craft tossing perilously in its wake, but hammering after it. Satan swerved his boat to the right, hoping he would be able to head off one of the murderous raiders.

A puff of smoke showed from the larger speedboat. Slim kept his glasses riveted on the boats, but he shouted: "They're firing at us from Simmiss' boats. Probably trying to warn us off."

The barge was scarcely a half mile away and the gangster's big craft was sweeping towards it. The Coast Guard cutter was veering out to challenge them. Satan could see men manning the guns on the cutter. In the background floated the barge, slow and bulky with its important cargo.

The gangsters' craft swirled close in front of Satan. He saw a man half-standing, with something clutched in one hand. He recognized it as dynamite.

"They're going to dynamite the barge!" Satan shouted. "They're going to try and blast the cars open!"

Slim whipped around, his eyes crazed with excitement. "Captain! Simmiss is in the smaller boat, with another man at the wheel! I can see him clearly!" He turned again, then suddenly ducked his head. "He's shooting at us."

"Let him," Satan howled back above the roar of the motors. "If he can hit us at this speed, he's better than I thought he was!"

A dull boom rose above the motor racket. The cutter was firing across the bow of the big speed boat.

But the man who held the stick of dynamite completed his throw.

Satan watched the thing arc high in the air, then fall short of its mark by perhaps thirty feet. A geyser of water shot high into the morning air from the impact of the explosive on the surface. The gangster boat whipped around at terrific speed. It sped past the cutter, then back up the other side.

Satan leaned close to Slim. "I got the plan! The men in the fast boat do the blasting. Simmiss' crazy hope is that the cars will be blasted open, that Pagan will hit the water in the general break, and that he will pick him up in the small boat!"

"He's crazy!" Slim howled.

"So am I!" Satan roared back. "Here goes! There's only two of us, but there's about two hundred souls on that barge that need protection!"

He swung the prow of his boat and streaked for the craft that carried the dynamiters. The barge was closer now.

"Open up your gat!" he shouted to Slim. "Let the Coast Guard know which side we're on, or they're liable to take a pot shot at us!"

The two boats rushed headlong at one another like runaway horses.

THE MEN in the gangsters' speedboat were firing. The whine of hot lead filed the air. A spidery web traced itself on the windshield in front of Satan. There was no sound—nothing above the hammering of the racing cylinders.

The dynamiter was rising in the pit again, lifting his arm to strike. The boat was so close to the barge that it seemed to Satan he couldn't miss. Satan thought of the terrific explosion that would follow—the number of lives that would be forfeited to this madman's lust for wealth and power. "Damn Simmiss and all of the rotten murderers that did his work!"

Now it was a test of speed and guts. Satan wrenched the wheel of his craft and rammed straight into the path of the dynamiters. He feared for a moment that he might force the dynamite-loaded boat into the barge, but he had to take the chance.

The gangsters could see him coming, like a sea monster riding out of hell. The water of the bay rose up in crazy cascade and Satan's hands were white upon the wheel. Now the dynamiter stood with the paralysis of fear governing his face. Satan drove his boat right up to the startled noses of Simmiss' gorillas. He wrenched mightily at the last moment and miraculously avoided a crack-up. In the tense moment, guns heated the air and spoke the hollow words of Death. Through it all Slim stood like a grim statue, his one hand braced to give him balance, his other hand servant to the eye that was on the pilot. Slim's gun spat.

"Got him! Got him!" the gaunt man roared. "I got the pilot!"

Satan turned his head... but the Simmiss speed boat disappeared behind him as if suddenly jerked by a taut cable.

"He cut his gun!" Slim shouted. "I potted him and he's out of it. They stopped!"

Satan stared, looking back over his shoulder as he gunned ahead faster. Three men were standing in the cockpit of that stalled craft, their hands raised high over their heads.

Satan looked around, his eyes seeking that other boat. He looked right and left. He found it, like a streak racing shoreward, veering to clear a ferry boat that was ambling like an old woman in hoop skirts.

"Simmiss is running for it!" he yelled. "Get set, Slim! We're going after him!"

Grimly, he slammed the throttle wide and nosed after the smaller boat. Satan's craft pulled up on it like an express train overhauling a trolley car. Simmiss looked back and saw them. He raised his left hand. More puffs of smoke grew from that boat. Slim opened fire, his gun hand resting on the deck of the leaping speedboat.

"Never get him that way, Slim. You haven't a chance," Satan shouted. "Wait 'til we're closer!"

The speedcraft rammed squarely for Simmiss', then veered off at the last minute. Again Satan wrenched the wheel and raced in a circle. The waves he caused slammed against Simmiss' craft.

Simmiss dropped down in his seat, clutching the deck for support. His boat was bobbing like a cork in a storm. Twice it keeled badly. The waves from the larger boat rocked it crazily. Satan held his wheel whipped in a circle. Simmiss' pilot yanked wildly at his wheel, trying to change his course.

And at that moment, a wave swept in on him from Satan's craft, a wave that caught him going in the same direction. The smaller boat went over.

"The boathook," Satan roared, cutting his throttle and jockeying his craft back into position. He gunned the boat around, then throttled slowly for the overturned craft.

Slim pulled the boathook loose from its rack on the deck in front of him, held it poised while Satan ranged up slowly. Two heads bobbed above water… one with hands clutching frantically. One head sank beneath the surface and the other remained. They recognized the head.

"It's Simmiss," Slim shouted.

The man was struggling to hold onto the hull of his boat, at the same time trying to raise his automatic with his left. Slim reached out and swung the boathook. He swung it once more. It caught in Simmiss's clothing.

"Hold it," he called to Satan. The boat steadied. Slim leaned far overside. He grunted with the effort and hauled hard.

Simmiss, unconscious and dripping water into the pit, was hauled aboard. Satan gunned the throttle full forward and turned in the direction of his dock.

"The last break for the jail-breaker," he said, with a cold smile. "For years, I suppose, Simmiss has been selling jail-breaks. Now I'll sell him one. His very last!"

CHAPTER 14
GUTS AND GUNS

SATAN GUIDED the boat on a beeline for its wharf, his eyes peeled for the Harbor Police. Slim had jammed the dripping Simmiss between himself and his chief.

"If we can make another four miles without any chase," Satan said, his eyes roving the shoreline, "I think we'll be safe."

"Maybe the cutter has radioed ashore?" Slim suggested in warning.

"I don't know," Satan said. "They certainly saw what side we were on. Maybe they think we're cops."

"I hope so," Slim grunted.

The air had its effect on Simmiss. Two minutes later, he jerked his head drunkenly, batted his eyes clear of the water and peered at Slim. Satan's gaunt lieutenant shifted his gun to his right hand, held it against the side of the cockpit.

After a moment, the snatch-king turned his head, his eyes dazed and seeking Satan's face. He gasped, and a scream of terror broke from his lips.

"You!" he screamed. *"You!"*

Satan smiled without looking around at the man. "Oh! You're awake, are you, Simmiss? That's good… because I want to talk business with you. How much money have you got with you?"

Simmiss licked his lips and glanced sideways at Slim. He hesitated a moment. "None," he said at last. "I don't carry it around with me."

Satan laughed. "You rat! You're too much of a chiseler to put a dime down long enough for it to get cold. Search him, Slim!"

Satan's lieutenant patted the man's overcoat pockets expertly, then savagely ripped the coat open. Buttons sprayed to the floor of the cockpit. "Raise your arms, you louse, or I'll kill you to make the job easier!"

Simmiss raised his arms, but his greenish eyes were ugly on Slim.

The search went on. The coat, the vest, the hip pockets. Suddenly Slim stopped, stared at the man with understanding dawning in his eyes.

"A money belt, huh?"

"No!" Simmiss screamed. He struggled to keep Slim's hands off him. But Slim pushed him away, slugged him with the butt of the gun. Simmiss wilted in his seat.

"What's your proposition?" he whispered, his eyes defeated. "You said you wanted to talk business?"

Satan tooled the boat shoreward on a long, diagonal slant. "First of all, Simmiss," he said. "Where is Siggy Murrah?"

"Dead," Simmiss snarled. *"Dead, dead, dead!"*

"You'll be deader than that if you don't talk," Satan told him. He turned slightly in his seat. "Slim—shoot him if he doesn't talk in five seconds!"

Slim started the count. "One—two—three—"

"It's you, Satan—you devil—I thought they'd done you in!"

"Murrah is on a boat headed for Trinidad," Simmiss snarled.

"What boat?"

"I won't tell. I won't tell, damn it!"

Slim belted the man in the mouth, raised the gun. He moaned, "On the *Queen of Trinidad*. Two days out."

"Good. Now—where's Phil Gilkane? And Sam Klami? We know Mikkle is in Mexico. Where in Mexico?"

"Mikkle is in Guadalajara, Mexico," Simmiss snapped. "Under the name of Lenster. I suppose you'll go shake him down now?"

"The others?"

"Klami is up in the Canadian Rockies. Gilkane, I don't know anything about."

"Sock him, Slim!"

"I swear I don't know about Gilkane! That was a break, not a spring." A touch of braggadocio came into the man's voice. "I do neat jobs."

Satin grinned slightly. "Like mine at the prison in New York? Simmiss—I want the names of the guards you bribed in the penitentiary."

"Oh, you want to work through them, too!"

"Give them to Slim. Memorize them, Slim."

"I got the stiffs through on the supply wagons," Simmiss said, sullenly. "Got the others out the same way. I knew you couldn't figure that one."

Satan twisted the wheel and headed for shore. The dock was two miles away. "All right, Simmiss. Now grab your money belt off and pass it over, and then you go to the police."

"What? And I go to the police? You mean, *or* I go to the police!"

"I said, *and* you go to the police," Satan said coldly. "If you don't turn it over, I'll kill you with my bare hands and take it from you."

Simmiss sat quiet, his eyes darting from one to the other of them. Then he laughed harshly. "God! After all this trouble, and planning. It would have come off, only for you, Satan. Imagine—" he laughed wildly, "I would have got another quarter million for turning Pagan Lorando in to his mob!"

Slim gasped. Satan turned his head, his eyes wide behind his goggles. "Another quarter million? You mean, you got a quarter million already, for the try?"

But Simmiss had seen his mistake. He grew silent, his face was purple.

"No wonder you raised so much hell out there to-day," Satan laughed grimly. "A cool half million for a half hour on the water. But you'd blow every man in the country to hell trying to get it, wouldn't you?"

Something seemed to snap inside that crazy brain of Simmiss'. The man surged up, tried to smash Satan. But Slim grappled with him. Satan's lieutenant raised his gun to shoot; but Simmiss was on him like a wildcat. He wrenched the thing loose from the gaunt man and turned it swiftly to Satan, who was trying to swing the boat clear from crashing the dock.

"Captain!" Slim screamed, throwing himself forward again.

But he was too late. Simmiss had the gun at Satan's head and pulled the trigger....

BUT THERE was only a dull click. The one chance in ten thousand had turned up to save Satan, for the moment—a defective bullet was in the chamber. Simmiss pulled again, and again, fought like a madman when Slim clawed at him. Satan swung sideways to smash the man with his fist.

But Slim had stopped suddenly, was jamming his hand into his inside pocket, under his overalls. He whipped it out again, then slammed it hard against the crazed man's neck. Simmiss collapsed with a gurgle, the blood starting from his neck and spurting in streams down his coat. The ivory handle of a knife protruded just above his collar.

Satan stared a moment, looked quickly at Slim, then away. He steered the boat into the dock.

"For—Big Bill," Slim said in a low voice.

Slim scrambled out on the dock and tied up the boat. He helped Satan lift the dying man to the wharf, then ran for some canvas to wrap him in. Swiftly, they carried the man to their car. Slim expertly stripped the money belt from the crook and strapped it about his own waist.

He slammed the rear door and Satan took the wheel, speeding to a secluded spot some miles down the road. He turned in there. Slim bundled Simmiss out of the car, laid him on the ground. He made a quick examination, then looked up at Satan.

"Practically gone now, Captain."

Satan stared at the man. "That's his freedom," he said quietly. "It's the only freedom he could ever know. Get out your pen and a piece of paper, Slim—and take this letter."

When his lieutenant was ready, Satan began:

To Mr. Jo Desher, Chief, F.B.I. He paused a minute. Then, *It seems we are destined to meet now and again, Desher. I can't say that I'm sorry you weren't in on this thing a bit faster; because you might have beat me to the satisfaction of nailing the toughest crook and murderer you or I ever ran up against. But—I give you the credit.*

He dictated the full story to Slim, giving all the details of the jail breaks. He told of Simmiss' methods, where the fugitives could be found, and the names of the crooked jail guards. When he had finished, he said: "Just sign it… Captain Satan."

They carried the dead Simmiss farther back in the woods and hid the tarpaulin-covered corpse effectively, sticking the letter that Slim had taken from Satan into the man's hand. Slim wiped the knife handle carefully.

On the way back to the city, Satan turned suddenly. "Slim! What hand did you write that letter with?"

"The left, naturally," Slim smiled. "I'm not that careless that I'd use my right hand for Jo Desher! I'll 'phone him just before we leave, right?"

THE EASTBOUND Transcontinental plane emptied its passengers at the Newark airport. Four of the passengers made an expertly swift and unobtrusive departure from the field, taking a taxi to Newark. There they climbed down and paid the driver. They walked two streets over and got into another cab.

This they took for ten miles, paying the cab driver off at a roadside restaurant. They ate sparsely, then summoned a private car from a nearby garage. They drove to the Jersey City terminal of the Courtland Street ferry, paid the driver and went aboard the next boat.

Satan took Slim aside. "I want you to go down personally to the warehouse and superintend the removal of that policeman and Nick Carfano. Ship the wax arm we took from Klami's grave to Jo Desher, in Washington. It'll be a nice souvenir for him.

"Strap Carfano to that copper," he continued. "It'll be some excuse for the poor cop for having been away for so long. Then, dump them out—gagged, of course—where they will be found within ten minutes. Clear out the warehouse; that cop may have a good memory. Move the stuff to the deserted East Side factory.

"How long will that take you?" he asked Slim finally.

Slim scratched his head. "Half an hour—if I can use Kayo."

Satan smiled suddenly. "I'm using Kayo and Pat myself. Do the best you can with Gentleman Dan and Soapy."

After the ferry had docked and Slim had gone, Satan called Pat and Kayo aside.

"How'd you fellows like a nice piece of fish?" he asked confidentially.

"Sure, I'd love it!" Pat said.

Kayo licked his chops. "That's just my dish!"

"All right! Now—I'll tell you what to do. Up the line a ways, on this street, there's a nice fishing tackle store open. Understand? Now— down the line away—" He moved closer. "Come nearer, boys! I can't shout this! Down the line away…"

Pat and Kayo listened to Satan with growing wonder in their eyes.

After their chief had shaken hands and left, Pat and Kayo stood irresolute on the corner, staring morosely up the street. Finally Kayo stirred and said, "Aw, come on, Pat! What the hell, I ain't fished in years. Anyway, the Aquarium is free admission—the way we work it."

Pat dusted his generous red mustache and growled, "Sure, it's you I've been waiting for all the time."

IT WAS past midnight. Two ghostly figures flitted around the great, domed building where every specie of fish was stored for a great city's curiosity. One of them paused, stared down into a tank. "Is this a swordfish?" he whispered.

"That's a seal, you mug!"

"Sure, and if those things sticking out of his mouth aren't swords, what are they?"

"Put the seat of your pants near them and find out! Come on!"

CHAPTER 15
SPORTSMAN'S RETURN

CARY ADAIR stretched his long legs luxuriously and yawned. "Another cup of coffee, please, Jeremy," he requested in a bored voice.

"Yes, Mr. Adair."

The tall, morose butler-chauffeur-valet moved swiftly and silently across the rich Turkish rug and wafted Adair's cup away. He was back in two seconds with it filled.

"How did you know I wanted another cup?" Adair asked, his gray eyes rebuking.

"I didn't, sir," Jeremy said mildly. "I had poured it already for myself, sir."

Adair added cream and sugar and stirred the coffee idly. He walked to the window and stared down at the view of New York Bay far below. The steady ring of the telephone sounded in the stillness of the room.

"The house telephone, sir," Jeremy murmured, sliding toward the instrument.

"I'm not in, Jeremy," Adair said.

Jeremy announced: "Mr. Adair's residence. Oh, yes, indeed, sir. He is in. Won't you come up?"

Adair turned from the window. "Jeremy! I told you—"

"Mr. Dresher, sir."

"Oh!"

The F.B.I. man swept into the room, his eyes beady in their concentration on Adair. "Where have you been?"

Adair blinked. Jeremy paused in mid-stride, his eyebrows expressing shocked surprise. "Why, that's a sweet greeting, Jo! I've been fishing, of course. You knew that."

Desher glowered at Adair, then at Jeremy. "Did I? Did I?" He whipped a handkerchief from his pocket, expertly unrolled an ivory handled knife that was wrapped there. "Ever see this before?"

Adair nodded, walked back to his coffee cup. He stirred it casually, took a leisurely sip. Then: "Of course I've seen it. Didn't

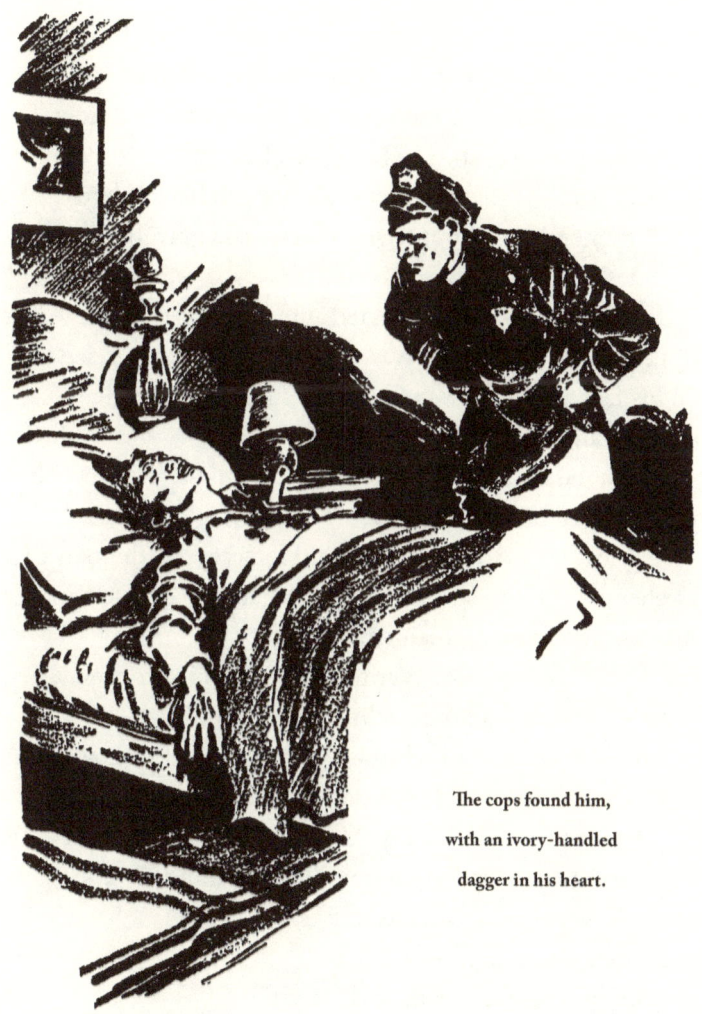

The cops found him,
with an ivory-handled
dagger in his heart.

some blighter toss it at you, right downstairs here? Don't tell me you're still looking for the man who did it!"

Desher gathered a rumbling cough deep in his throat. "Got anything to show for your fishing trip?" he asked challengingly. He set the knife on the table and faced Adair squarely.

"Jeremy. Show Mr. Desher those beautiful swordfish we nipped. And the marlin! That *is* a whopper. Isn't it, Jeremy?"

"A tremendous whopper, sir," Jeremy said gravely. "This way, Mr. Desher."

The two of them disappeared into the pantry while Adair sipped his coffee. Desher was out in a moment, a puzzled look on his face. He refused coffee. He refused a drink. He refused a cigar. But he did want something.

"Cary," he said with an attempt at heartiness. "I've never had your autograph, have I? Or Jeremy's? I'd like to have them both."

"A pleasure," Adair murmured. He accepted the pen that Desher passed him, started to sign his name on a piece of paper that the F.B.I. man presented.

"Wait!" Desher said. "Write something nice for me, Cary. Like—'I give you all the credit in the world.'"

Adair raised polite eyebrows. "A modest little fellow, aren't you?" But he wrote and signed as directed.

"Desher turned to Jeremy. "You, too."

Jeremy made him a slight bow. "Do you mind my asking my master's permission, Mr. Desher?"

Desher was triumphant.

"Oh! So you don't want to do it, eh?"

Jeremy took the pen in his right hand and wrote the required words.

Desher snatched the paper up and looked at it—his face

falling ten degrees each second. He managed a strangled, "Thank you." Then he turned to Adair. "I will have a cup of coffee, Cary. And a cigar. I'd like to sit a minute."

He had finished his second cup when a thought struck him; struck him so forcibly that he wrenched around in his chair and looked over his right shoulder. "Where's that knife?" he barked.

"Knife?" Jeremy asked politely. Adair blinked. Desher whirled to the other side of his chair.

"Ouch!" he roared. "What the—?"

He reached a hand behind him and pulled the ivory handled blade into view, then vigorously rubbed the seat of his pants.

"I don't remember putting that there," he said.

After the cigar, Desher joined Adair at the window and they stood staring down at the bay. Suddenly the F.B.I. man craned his neck, peered at the Aquarium far below.

"Wonder what all those cops are doing down there?"

Adair stirred. Jeremy coughed discreetly in the background. "Probably kiddies day, or something," Adair yawned. "What does ever go on down in that place, anyway. Nothing surprising, would you say?"

Desher guffawed. "I'd say it would be a lot more sensible for you to go look at a swordfish there than go all the way to Florida to catch one! What a life, what a life! And me a hard working man."

AFTER THE F.B.I. chief had gone, Adair said to Jeremy: "Have that Marlin mounted and send it to Mr. Desher, with my compliments. Have a plate made. A brass plate, you know,

with his name and mine. Send him a letter to-day, about it."
He smiled slightly.

"You might add a P.S., Jeremy—Say: *'Wasn't it pretty out there on the bay this morning!'* "